Six Ways to Sunday
From Faith through Doubt to Truth

Six Ways to Sunday
From Faith through Doubt to Truth

Jay Lee

To the seekers on the path ahead of me.
Thank you for finding. And sharing.

CONTENTS

Prologue

He stopped. How many times had he tried to tell her? He had wanted to, he had rehearsed it over and over in his mind. If he was hesitating now, that was understandable. How could he tell the one person he cherished most, needed most, the one he most wanted to protect from the very hard truth he now owed her?

He rested his hand on the desk in his den, beside which he had just knelt in prayer. A tough, necessary prayer. Now, feet still glued to the floor, he lifted his eyes to the bookshelf above. This was where he kept his personal library, his hobby reading. His C.S. Lewis collection, fairly worn but probably not worn enough, was next to a small clutch of books about Central American temples and history. They were right below his collection of World War II books, which in turn were right below his journals.

Journaling had once been something of a passion, maybe an obsession. As a younger man he had had so many ideas that he had needed to explore. His journals were the place he could record his aspirations, his misgivings, and his most profound moments.

Most prized among all his journals was the one that chronicled that summer. Nearly twenty years now, that summer was the one. It was in that summer that everything fell into alignment, everything made sense, but only after it first threatened to wreck him completely. There had been so much to write about! And write he did, nearly every day.

He took his hand from the desk and retrieved the journal from that long-ago summer, half a lifetime away. He turned through the pages until he found it, the day where everything began.

Chapter 1

Sunday, May 31, 1987

It has only been a day since I wrote, but, man, I'm really stuck on something. Can't sleep, can't think. Can't believe this is getting to me. I have to figure this out. Maybe I just need to bury it.

"Andy, you look terrible."

He looked terrible because he felt terrible. It wasn't just the lack of sleep – he'd spent the whole night pacing his dorm room, which he had all to himself because the summer term was starting and most other students had gone home or on vacation or anywhere but here. Not Andy. He had nowhere else to go, which was fine with him. The chance to work with Dr. Gordon over the summer was worth it. The man was a legend in his field, and the rare academic who was also an open believer.

"Sorry, professor, I didn't get much sleep last night," he offered. It was more than a bit of an understatement. He hadn't even managed to lie down for five minutes, much less sleep that many. He sat down in the chair at the edge of Gordon's desk, exhausted.

"Are you not feeling well?" Professor Gordon asked. He wasn't looking at Andy anymore, instead he scanned through some papers he had in a file folder in front of him, a few academic journals spread open on his desk. Surely he was asking to be polite, the way anybody asks if you've had a good day, not necessarily interested in an answer. He wasn't the classic model of the messy, absentminded professor, but he could get pretty engrossed in his work, the work that drew Andy to be his research assistant in the first place.

"I'm fine," Andy responded so as to dismiss any attention and let Gordon dive into the day's work, eventually involving Andy in some library research or searching the new Lexis/Nexis service at the law library. Despite the troubling night Andy had had, he didn't want it to get in the way of his work for Professor Gordon.

Something Gordon heard in Andy's voice must have alerted him to the real answer because he paused, set down his papers, turned to gaze directly into Andy's bleary eyes and summarized the truth of it. "No, you're not."

Andy glanced down and Gordon leaned in a bit, pursing his lips in a questioning frown, "What happened?"

Andy shrugged. He felt a sudden wave of emotion welling up in him which he tried to dismiss. Tears nearly formed in his eyes, he tried to blink them away, mostly successfully. He realized he couldn't hide what he was dealing with, but how could he share it? How could he possibly explain that one simple question had brought him to his knees? This man in front of him, a man of wisdom, of faith, surely he would be embarrassed to find out that Andy had been so easily shaken.

But he had. By a single question.

You don't really believe that, do you?

It had been an effortless question, a snide comment tossed out in such clear contempt for the possibility of belief that it had shut him down completely. In the moment, he had managed a shrug and a mumbled, "I dunno," but for the rest of the evening and then all through the night, the question haunted him.

Did he really believe that? And if he did, what did that make him? And if he didn't, well, what then? What else didn't he believe? That was what the visiting lecturer – a pastor – had said: If you doubt this, what else do you doubt? It was the closing argument of his lecture and it seemed to make a lot of sense to Andy. Until while walking to the dorms his classmate Jerry made fun of the man that they had been required to listen to for their history class. Then, seeing that Andy wasn't ready to joke along, Jerry tossed out the provoking question. In a moment, Andy was suddenly forced to see things in a new light. He saw a new choice, one that had never seemed real to him before: was he going to be a believer or a nonbeliever?

The thought that he was suddenly so close to becoming a nonbeliever felt devastating to him. As if he was standing on the edge of an abyss, about to toss himself into the chasm below. How could he feel capable of denying the faith he had grown up with, had felt his whole life – had even felt a bit superior because of it – and now here he was, on the verge of admitting that he wasn't sure what he believed?

All of that hung over him like a great weight and Professor Gordon seemed to sense it.

"Andy, whatever it is, it's not going away on its own. So let's have it, what happened?"

Shrugging again seemed like too much effort for too little reward, so instead, Andy just sighed and answered with a question.

"Do you believe Jonah was swallowed by a whale?"

Gordon was physically startled by the question, pushed back in his chair. His face grew tight as he regarded the student in front of him, seeing him in a new light, but what light Andy did not know.

"Hmm. Mmmm-mmmm," he muttered in contemplation. Finally, Gordon stood up, closed his file folder, tucking it under his arm. Then he reached to the bookshelf above his desk, seeking something. Locating it, he took it from the shelf, then looked down at Andy.

"I've been in this office since dawn, too long already. Let's go for a walk."

Relieved that maybe Gordon was just going to drop it, Andy pulled his backpack on his shoulder and followed the older man out the office door, closing it behind him.

~

They stepped outside of the College of Arts and Sciences, on the side facing Comm Ave toward the Mugar Chapel. It was a lovely first of June, the sun was shining and the coeds were starting to come out for their morning activities. The few joggers were already coming back from their morning runs, sporting their Walkman tape players and pony tails. It was a bright, beautiful day in every way except on the inside, where Andy was harboring an ugly darkness.

Andy's hope that Gordon would drop it was soon dashed as the professor spoke up.

"Tell me, does this have anything to do with last night's guest pastor?"

"Yes."

"I thought so."

They walked a space in silence.

"He's quite a figure, isn't he? A man of great faith."

"I guess so."

"You guess so?"

"No, I think so, it's just that the whole time I was listening, I was going along with what he was saying and it all made sense. Until—"

"Until what?"

"Until afterward, when I, or rather, when my friend whose also in Darby's 322 history class, started making fun of him."

"On what grounds?"

"Jonah and the whale."

They walked some more in silence as Gordon thought this over.

"I see. Hence your question."

"Yes."

It felt good to get this basic scenario off his chest, even if he knew he couldn't fully explain why this one moment troubled him so.

"And you want to know if I believe that Jonah was swallowed by a whale because..." Gordon left it as a pause, but it was clearly a question.

"Because, I don't know, maybe it would make it easier for me to believe."

"Is that what you want?"

"What?"

"Do you want it to be easy to believe?"

"I don't know."

"Because if you want it to be easy to believe, you've come to the wrong place."

Andy looked around at the hustle and bustle of the busy street, the Boston University campus located right in the middle of the metropolis, all the energy around him.

"You mean Boston?"

"No, though that's an interesting question in itself. The liberal academic environment, not to mention the self-indulgence of college life, none of it is designed to make it easier to believe."

"That's for sure. But what place did you mean?"

"I meant earth."

This silenced Andy and Professor Gordon both, for different reasons. They continued this way, on past the library where the professor finally spoke.

"Andy, let me ask you an important question before we begin."

"Begin?"

"Yes, we're about to start something here, you and I. Or, you already started it, I'm going to help you finish it."

"Okay, shoot."

"What is faith?"

Andy shuffled a bit, his hands in his pockets, feeling like the question was some kind of test, a test he wasn't sure he could pass. He offered the only thing he knew how.

"Faith is the substance of things hoped for, but not seen."

A smile came across Gordon's face. "Paul to the Hebrews. A safe answer."

"I guess so."

"Do you have faith?"

Again, Andy felt aware of a test he was not sure he could pass. Maybe today least of all.

"I think so. I mean I did think so. And maybe once I finally get some sleep I'll feel like I do again. But right now I'm not sure."

"Good," professor Gordon nodded, pursing his lips and knitting his brow in satisfied contemplation.

"Good? How is that good? I know most people come to college come to get away from their faith, I came here – I chose to work with you – because I want to keep my faith!" Now Andy was starting to feel alive with worry and doubt, he wasn't sure the professor understood the gravity of the situation.

"No, Andy, you don't want to keep your faith." Gordon said, seeming unfazed by Andy's protestations. "You want to improve it."

"All due respect, professor, but I'm not sure that's what I'm doing. One day my faith is strong and I'm going along just fine, the next day a single question about a single story casts my whole understanding of my faith – myself, even – into doubt." His heart was racing as he said it, even though it felt good to put it in this dramatic of relief.

"That's because you're ready to go beyond faith. You're ready to be set free."

Set free? Andy didn't want to be disrespectful, but this airy statement seemed more like Philosophy 101 than spiritual guidance, spinning him further around a carousel of questioning, always moving but getting nowhere. By now he was feeling sick inside, physically ill. He had asked a simple question: Did Professor Gordon really believe that Jonah was swallowed by a whale? Surely this was an easy question to answer. It had taken some courage to even ask it but he hoped that by doing so he would get an answer and be able to put the concerns of the night before to rest. Yet so far, instead of answers he'd gotten riddles and puzzles, moving him faster and faster around the carousel. As he felt his pulse surge and his anxiety levels rise, he wanted desperately to ask if he could just get off. The only thing that kept him in place was the steeling, assuring presence of Professor Gordon.

The professor, as if he perceived the turmoil enveloping Andy, finally addressed what Andy thought was the meat of the issue.

"Andy, you asked a fair question and I haven't given you the answer. That's because the answer you seek is not the right one. You want me to confirm your faith and tell you that everything is all right, you want me, whether you know it or not, to take the burden of doubt from your mind."

That's exactly what I want! Andy thought, realizing that even as he sought it, he wasn't going to get it.

Gordon continued. "But I won't do that. Not because I can't. And if you were a ten-year-old boy asking me this question I might be tempted to give you an easy – but temporary – answer. But you're not. You're a man. A man of faith, who is ready to go beyond faith."

"What does that mean?"

"You are ready to go from faith, through doubt, to truth."

Truth. The word seemed to fit like a puzzle piece into a specific spot in Andy's mind and despite his lack of sleep and current confusion, it fit well. Then he realized it, the reason it fit was because just seconds before, Gordon had opened up the space for it in his mind with something he had said: *You are ready to be set free.*

"Because truth is what sets us free."

"Well done. Very well done. This just may work after all."

~

Stephen Tentworthy, the controversial pastor had lectured Sunday evening in the School of Theology, an invited guest of various professors, none of whom respected the man. But all of whom, curiously, felt the need to have him speak on campus nearly every year, in what was evident show of the open dialogue they believed was necessary in the religious life of a secular campus. An open dialogue that was really a way to invite conservative religious views to the campus so that in later classes they could be undermined using a more secular viewpoint. Andy had known this going in – he was not unaware of BU's reputation. And he'd spent two years taking courses in everything from biology to art history to human health – otherwise known as sex education – all of which seemed to erode faith and hold it up first as an object of pity, leading eventually to derision. That was outside the School of Theology and was probably common in most liberal universities, Andy surmised. The surprise to him had been how little difference there was inside the School of Theology.

That one of the country's oldest schools of theology – it was the founding college of what was by now Boston University – had grown up to house a faculty comprised largely of secular humanists, meant that very few of their religion courses were taught by actual believers. That is, people who believed in the divine sonship of Jesus Christ. Some thought Jesus was a special teacher, others taught that he was divinely inspired, but most generally concluded that the whole Son of God story was myth, though for some, it was a benign and even beneficial myth. Dr. Gordon was one of the exceptions to the rule, although his position was held in the history department, not the School of Theology. Because his specialty was history of American Christianity, he had many connections to the people in the theology school.

That was what drew Andy to Boston University. It was Professor Gordon's extensive writings on the history of Christianity and the unique vibrancy that characterized the American experience of Jesus, that made Andy want to be a historian. To spend your life reading about the faithful across history and writing and lecturing about the legacy they left – it was nearly a religious calling for him and studying under Dr. Gordon would mean he had the best shot at doing exactly what he felt compelled to do.

What he hadn't counted on was how messy it could get. Boston was a wonderful city, he half expected to try to settle here after graduation. So much education, so much culture – and even though he wasn't originally a Red Sox fan, living through last season being just blocks away from Fenway Park was nothing short of magical. If only Buckner hadn't let that ball between his legs, maybe the curse of the Bambino would have been lifted!

But if life in Boston had been a plus for this Iowa-born boy, university life had been taxing. When he turned down the offer to study history at Southern Methodist University in order to come to BU, he had imagined that the differences would be modest. Sure, the kids at BU would do more drugs, have more sex, and be more vulgar than those at SMU. But he didn't realize he would feel like he was drowning under the weight of it, occasionally surfacing to gasp for clean air before being dragged back down under.

The promise of becoming an assistant to Professor Gordon is what caused him to hold out. Andy enrolled in his Intro to Christian History class, technically a 300-level class designed for juniors, when he was just a sophomore. The work was challenging, but invigorating. And, make no excuses, he brown-nosed his way into Gordon's inner circle, asking questions after class, doing outside reading so he'd sound as smart as a junior. And it worked. Late in that semester Gordon took him aside and asked him what his major was going to be.

"American history," he beamed proudly.

"That's a noble cause," the professor said. "But why the interest in Christianity?"

Andy had no idea – could not have even imagined – that Gordon had seen through him early on in the semester and could tell he was practically auditioning for the research assistant slot. So he kept auditioning.

"Because I'm a believer, professor, and I want to spend my life really getting into this topic."

Gordon regarded him with stifled amusement. It hadn't been a risk to divulge that he was a believer, not to Gordon, who wrote openly about his own faith, considering it an obligation to his academic readers that he disclose his own personal viewpoint. This was in contrast to the supposed objectivity that the atheists and agnostics writing in the same field claimed they had toward the subject.

"Well, young believer. I think I have a job for you if you really mean it," Gordon finally said with a sincere smile.

Andy spent the second semester of his sophomore year recording grades, taking attendance, and managing some of the details of Gordon's fairly rigorous research schedule. At any point he was sending manuscripts to this or that journal, receiving inquiries from academics around the world, and Andy soon found himself delivering letters from some of the most important thinkers in his field. Occasionally Gordon would share them with him.

It was exactly where he, a young man of evident faith, wanted to be. Which made him feel a bit invincible when he, now entering the summer term en route to becoming a bona fide junior, walked over to the School of Theology to hear Stephen Tentworthy's annual rant against the liberal university view of religion.

Tentworthy's firebrand style was precisely what the sponsoring faculty wanted. It was a style of preaching that hadn't been common in New England probably since the Second Great Awakening or maybe during the abolitionist movement propelled by Christian societies prior to the Civil War. There was so much brimstone in his preaching that he condemned sinners to hell on at least four occasions during his speech. Andy had to admit that made him feel a little uncomfortable, being uncertain where he stood on the question of hell and who will go there. Overall the speech had its intended effect: It demonstrated the dogmatic and unyielding approach of conservative religious thinkers.

What surprised Andy was not that the liberal students – most of them history or American studies majors who were required to attend for various summer classes they were taking – found the lecture laughable. Instead, the surprise to Andy was how much of it he enjoyed. Tentworthy had such a clear perspective on things: Good was good, evil was evil, and you should never play with the fire of hell unless you want to be consumed by it!

It was in the middle of criticizing modern scholarly interpretations of the bible – warning those who argued that the world was created in anything other than six days – that Tentworthy chose to zero in on the one story that had since then occupied Andy's mind and soul: Jonah.

"God gave us the story of Jonah as a test!" Tentworthy exclaimed, extending a long finger and leaning against the pulpit, causing the lights above him to cast shadows down his bony face as his brow dipped forward.

"'Let them see if they will believe!' God said, and so far, the modern world has failed the test. The story of Jonah is a test of our faith in God's ability to find us, to hunt us down when we oppose Him. That no matter how much we run from Him, He can find us. For in

Him is all power! He controls the waves and the winds, He controls even the fishes of the sea."

"I don't care if science tells us that a man cannot live inside the belly of a fish for three days. Science will also tell us that Moses could not part the Red Sea or that Jesus could not rise again after the grave. If we disbelieve Jonah, what else do we disbelieve? Do we not disbelieve the very Son of God Himself?"

It was a line of thinking that moved Andy, one he had never considered before. The very soul inside him wanted to stand and exclaim, I believe in all of it, because in that moment, he did believe in all of it, or was willing to, if that's what God required of him.

The talk so moved him that he told his classmate Jerry he wanted to thank Tentworthy in person afterward.

"Say what, for real? What, so you can get an autograph?" Jerry stammered.

"It'll only be a sec," Andy said, moving to the front of the quickly emptying room.

Some host faculty were standing around Tentworthy, thanking him for coming, smugly thinking that Tentworthy had done their job for them. Teaching the students that conservative religious thought was an oxymoron was going to be child's play after this. Which is perhaps why it surprised all of them to see the earnest young student leaning forward to interrupt, hand extended to Tentworthy.

"Pastor Tentworthy," he reached out, "I wanted to thank you for coming to preach to us tonight."

Tentworthy was himself surprised to see a student; likely he was aware of his role in the plans of his hosts. He returned Andy's outstretched hand with a firm handshake and piercing gaze. "You're welcome, son. Tell me, what's your name?"

"Andy, Andy Harding."

"Well, Andy, why do you think you're the only student here who has come to thank me?"

Suddenly uncomfortable, Andy demurred and only shook his head.

"Because this is the way it will be in the last days. Just as Lot could not find even one believer in Sodom and Gomorrah, so will Boston become a den of iniquity. You will only escape it by believing in every word God gives you through holy scripture."

Andy swallowed. The man's words were intense yet somehow compelling.

"Just remember: Jonah is your warning. If you can't believe Jonah, you can't believe Jesus."

And with that, the man broke the handshake, nodded, and turning to his hosts, left for the faculty door.

More than a bit disoriented but strangely alive, Andy turned, thinking this over. *If you can't believe Jonah, you can't believe Jesus.* He had never heard this before, had never considered it. It felt, at least at first, like an empowering statement. *Of course I can believe Jonah, of course I can believe Jesus.*

By the time Andy got outside, Jerry was already lighting a cigarette. It was already evening and a slight wind was coming from the north, across the river from Cambridge and an impatient Jerry clearly wanted to get back to the dorms.

"Man, what did he say to you?" Jerry joked. "Did he damn you, too?" he asked, laughing.

"No, he did the opposite, in fact. He told me I was the only one who was going to be saved." Andy was joking back, but his tone wasn't very light and Jerry possibly took it personally.

"Oh, so I'm damned and you're saved, how's that?"

"Because I believe in Jonah."

Jerry guffawed. "You're kidding, that's all it takes? That's, like, so easy I could even do it."

Jerry took a big drag from his cigarette and then added, almost conspiratorially, "Although it wouldn't be worth it. That Jonah is one whale of a fish story." He laughed, ejecting the rest of the tobacco smoke from his lungs, then coughing to try to add life to such an obvious pun.

Andy wasn't laughing. He didn't expect Jerry to believe in Jonah. He was pretty sure he didn't believe in Jesus, even though he was Catholic and all. But having Jerry call it out like that was uncomfortable, to say the least.

"I don't know, I think it teaches us a lot."

"Well, like, sure, of course it teaches us a lot," Jerry said, suddenly serious beyond his years. "Like any good fable teaches us a lot. But it's not *true*. I mean, nobody was actually swallowed by a whale and then puked up a few days later on the beach."

Andy didn't answer, not knowing whether he preferred the joking Jerry or the one who was of a sudden interested in pursuing this topic. That's when he said it.

"You don't really believe that, do you?"

It should have been a simple question, and had Andy not invited the more serious tone, maybe it wouldn't have struck him with such force as it did. But in that single moment Andy felt vulnerable in a way he hadn't before.

Did he believe Jonah? And if he didn't, what else didn't he believe?

Chapter 2

"Tell me exactly how he said it," Professor Gordon asked, pulling a scrap of paper out from the folder he had brought along and readying himself to write as Andy spoke.

"'You don't really believe that, do you?'" Andy quoted.

"No, sorry, not that part, that I got. I mean, tell me exactly what Tentworthy said about Jonah."

Andy had just finished recounting the entire story to Gordon while they sat on BU Beach, the inappropriately named stretch of grass above Storrow Drive that years before had actually sloped down to the Charles River and so retained its name. They had stopped there when the professor had asked Andy to tell him the whole experience from beginning to end.

Now, seated on the grass, Andy was a bit conflicted. In retelling it, it hadn't seemed as big as his night of sleeplessness made it feel. He was starting to think it was something he would just get over if he left it alone and he nearly regretted that he had mentioned it to Professor Gordon to begin with.

And maybe it would just pass, with some time and some sleep. But as it was, he had the world's foremost expert on American Christianity sitting down on the grass with him to reflect on a personal experience with American Christianity and he owed it to the man to answer his question.

"It was something like, 'The story of Jonah is a test of our faith in God's ability to find us, to hunt us down when we oppose Him.'" The words came haltingly and he had to kind of pick his way through, but he continued, "'That no matter how much we run from Him, He can find us. For in Him is all power! He controls the waves and the winds,

He controls even the fishes of the sea. I don't care if science tells us that a man cannot live inside the belly of a fish for three days. Science will also tell us that Moses could not part the Red Sea or that Jesus could not rise again after the grave. If we disbelieve Jonah, what else do we disbelieve? Do we not disbelieve the very Son of God himself?'"

Gordon wrote quickly, pencil extending the letters in the elegant script of someone who had spent many years studying handwritten manuscripts from a pre-mechanical type era. Then, without comment, he began erasing, first here, then there. Then he started writing some more, drawing marks and annotations. Andy had seen this before, it was the way the professor edited his manuscripts, always first by hand before ever committing them to a typewriter, or more recently, to WordPerfect on one of the department IBM-PCs with Andy's help.

When he finished, he handed the sheet of paper to Andy. On it was written:

Tentworthy's Dilemma:

The story of Jonah is a test of our faith in God's ability to find us, to hunt us down when we oppose Him. That no matter how much we run from Him, He can find us. For in Him is all power! He controls the waves and the winds, He controls even the fishes of the sea. Did Moses part the Red Sea? Could Jesus rise again after the grave? If we disbelieve Jonah, do we not disbelieve the very Son of God himself?

After he read it, Andy looked up at Gordon expectantly. The man was excited, nodding slightly, obviously thinking further down the path than Andy could see.

"Andy, I'm going to tell you something that I want you to accept uncritically for now. Understand?"

"Sure."

"What Tentworthy said, at least as I have edited it slightly here, is true."

Andy was confused. This was the very statement that had set him on edge and he was hoping that Gordon would tell him it was all wrong or something, that maybe it was just as easy as dismissing Tentworthy, thus undoing the logical knot he was tied up in. But now Gordon was telling him it was true.

It did not feel like this would set him free.

"But," Gordon added, only after letting Andy stew, possibly testing his resolve, "it is true in ways that you cannot see right now."

Gordon set himself to making some more notes on another piece of paper, his eyes squinting as if seeing a great distance.

Some time passed and Andy wondered what was next.

"Professor Gordon? Are we doing any research today?"

"Of course we are," the professor said, still writing.

"What are we researching?"

"Why, the story of Jonah, of course."

~

Now the word of the Lord came unto Jonah the son of Amittai, saying,

Arise, go to Nineveh, that great city, and cry against it; for their wickedness is come up before me.

But Jonah rose up to flee unto Tarshish from the presence of the Lord, and went down to Joppa; and he found a ship going to Tarshish: so he paid the fare thereof, and went down into it, to go with them unto Tarshish from the presence of the Lord.

But the Lord sent out a great wind into the sea, and there was a mighty tempest in the sea, so that the ship was like to be broken.

Then the mariners were afraid, and cried every man unto his god, and cast forth the wares that were in the ship into the sea, to lighten it of them. But Jonah was gone down into the sides of the ship; and he lay, and was fast asleep.

So the shipmaster came to him, and said unto him, What meanest thou, O sleeper? arise, call upon thy God, if so be that God will think upon us, that we perish not.

And they said every one to his fellow, Come, and let us cast lots, that we may know for whose cause this evil is upon us. So they cast lots, and the lot fell upon Jonah.

Then said they unto him, Tell us, we pray thee, for whose cause this evil is upon us; What is thine occupation? and whence comest thou? what is thy country? and of what people art thou?

And he said unto them, I am an Hebrew; and I fear the Lord, the God of heaven, which hath made the sea and the dry land.

Then were the men exceedingly afraid, and said unto him, Why hast thou done this? For the men knew that he fled from the presence of the Lord, because he had told them.

Then said they unto him, What shall we do unto thee, that the sea may be calm unto us? for the sea wrought, and was tempestuous.

And he said unto them, Take me up, and cast me forth into the sea; so shall the sea be calm unto you: for I know that for my sake this great tempest is upon you.

Nevertheless the men rowed hard to bring it to the land; but they could not: for the sea wrought, and was tempestuous against them.

Wherefore they cried unto the Lord, and said, We beseech thee, O Lord, we beseech thee, let us not perish for this man's life, and lay not upon us innocent blood: for thou, O Lord, hast done as it pleased thee.

So they took up Jonah, and cast him forth into the sea: and the sea ceased from her raging.

Then the men feared the Lord exceedingly, and offered a sacrifice unto the Lord, and made vows.

Now the Lord had prepared a great fish to swallow up Jonah. And Jonah was in the belly of the fish three days and three nights.

Andy looked over it again. The complete first chapter of the book of Jonah from the Old Testament in the Bible. He had copied the whole thing down in his journal, taking it from the King James Version, mostly because it was Gordon's favorite translation. "I don't read modernized Shakespearean verse just to make it easier to understand," he was known to say, "why would I read modernized Biblical English just to make it easier to understand?" Though in saying so he was being less than genuine because he had researched many translations of the Bible in his own writings and was fond of several of them depending on the purposes to which one was putting scripture.

Gordon had asked him to go home and copy the amended statement of Tentworthy's Dilemma, as he was calling it. "Put it in your journal. Then copy the first chapter of Jonah underneath it. We'll start there."

The *we* in that statement turned out to be a little white lie, as Gordon was laying out the tasks that he would have Andy do for the rest of Monday.

"You have some work to do today before we convene again later this afternoon. Can you come back at four o'clock?"

That's when Gordon handed Andy the second sheet of paper he had been writing on. Now that he'd completed copying the first chapter of Jonah into his journal, he pulled out that paper again and read the three steps it contained, copying each to his journal in turn:

1 – Find the word whale in the book of Jonah.

2 – Find the world's record for the longest someone has ever held their breath.

3 – Find the literal meaning of the word "literal."

The first step was going to be the easiest. Turning open his bible, Andy paged once again to the book of Jonah. To be honest with himself, even though he knew the story, it wasn't a scripture he had read much. It hadn't seemed very relevant to his life, not until Tentworthy's dilemma had made it suddenly so pressing the night before.

And what's more, until he copied the first chapter down word for word earlier that day, Andy hadn't even realized that the book of Jonah, for all that people know and retell the story, was only four chapters long, barely a couple of pages in his old King James edition of the Bible. Yet this little story had managed to stand out to so many people for so many years. Poring over the words, Andy set about to find the world whale.

As he skimmed, he mentally noted the structure of the tale: Chapter one tells the story of Jonah's call to preach to Nineveh and his urgent flight by boat away from Nineveh, basically heading in exactly the opposite direction where he is stopped by a storm and ultimately volunteers to be cast overboard to save the rest of the crew. Chapter two is something of a psalm, Andy noted, a prayer offered by Jonah to admit to his mistake and agree to comply with what God commanded him. In chapter three, Jonah delivers God's message of repentance to Nineveh, expecting that they won't believe him, yet they do, and the whole kingdom repents and is saved. In chapter four, Jonah pouts. That was really the only way Andy could describe it to himself. Jonah pouts, he's mad that God is going easy on the people of Nineveh. This one Andy couldn't quite deal with, but reflecting back on the task at hand – he was supposed to be looking for the word *whale* – he returned to the first two chapters where it was most likely to occur.

And there he found…nothing. He read and re-read to be sure, but it became clear very quickly that even though the whale figures prominently in the tale as his fellow believers tell it, in the book of Jonah itself the whale isn't even a whale – it's a fish and it's mentioned in precisely three verses: The last verse of chapter one and the first and the last verse of chapter two.

A fish?

Trying to get one step ahead of Professor Gordon, Andy thought this through. Why would this matter to the professor? The difference was just a word, it didn't really change the story. It's not like the scripture actually said submarine instead of whale. Though *that* would have solved the problem immediately.

At the same time, Andy felt a little embarrassed. How could the world *whale* appear nowhere in the book of Jonah yet he didn't realize it until he was forced to look for it? As a believer, shouldn't he have known what the scripture actually said?

He finally gave in and made a note in his journal next to the first task:

1 – Find the word whale in the book of Jonah. It isn't in there.

Then he turned to the second task, finding out how long anyone had ever held their breath. This one was easy enough, he thought, as he bundled up his journal and notes so he could head over to the bookstore in Kenmore Square where he figured he could thumb through a copy of the latest Guinness Book of World Records.

It was a few short blocks down Comm Ave to get to the campus bookstore, he figured he could stop at the pizza joint next door for a bite to eat. As he pulled the door open, the heat of the pizza oven spilled out, pushing gently against him. Pulling him the other way was the smell of pepperoni and a glimpse of one of the girls waiting in line to buy a slice. It was Christine, a junior from Gordon's class, the one Andy had been the TA for. She was finely featured, a porcelain beauty whose light curls framed her flawless face. Andy slowly stepped into line a few spaces behind her, wondering if he dared try to make eye contact. She would know who he was, sure, he had handed her papers back to her the whole semester long, but would she acknowledge him outside of class? He wasn't sure she would and he wasn't sure he dared find out the hard way that his suspicion was right.

He sat there pretending not to notice her, though it was ridiculous to imagine not noticing her. The thought of hiding from her while desperately wanting to talk to her made him begin to blush, even as he tried in vain to pretend the blush was just an aftereffect of the heat of the pizza oven in the cramped space.

Soon she was ordering her slice and then stepping back, an action which made her turn her head his direction. Though he tried to pretend he didn't see her, their eyes crossed paths and even in his supreme embarrassment, Andy couldn't imagine pretending he hadn't recognized her. He began a grin, one that was hopefully small enough that if she pretended not to see him, he wouldn't have overextended himself.

What happened next nearly caused his knees to buckle. At the first glance in his direction, she smiled – that perfect smile – and looking right at him, she beamed.

"Andy!" she said, moving toward him.

"Um, hi," he responded, trying to act like her impending arrival in his immediate vicinity wasn't going to be one of highlights of his day, possibly his week.

"I didn't know you were here this summer," she started, so comfortable and easy in her skin. She was in white shorts, her thin legs dangling down until they terminated in canvas sneakers, those sneakers stepping his way. He tried his hardest not to notice how perfect her legs were.

"Yeah, I am, all summer."

"Great, I'm here at least first summer term. I'm trying to do a semester abroad next winter, but to graduate on time I gotta finish some of my major requirements, so I'm here trying to get ahead of my schedule. How about you?"

"Huh?" He wasn't sure what she was asking, or partly he wasn't sure why she would be interested at all.

"You trying to get ahead of graduation, too?"

"Graduation?" Saying it out loud helped him realize that she didn't know he was only finishing his sophomore year. And in that moment he would have done anything to change the subject so that she would not realize he was younger than she was. But there was no way out of this one.

"No, not me. I'm taking a few classes, but I'm mostly here to work for Prof Gordon."

"Oh, yeah? That's rad. Making good money?"

"Not really, no, but American history's my thing so I'm hoping to learn a lot from him."

"He's really smart, isn't he?"

"Definitely smart."

He couldn't believe his good fortune that she was even spending more than a *hello* on him and worried that he wouldn't know how to make the conversation last as long as possible, something he desperately desired since it was now probably going to be the highlight of his month. His turn to order a slice came up, he asked for two pepperonis, anticipating the oily goodness of this staple of his culinary life.

"Thanks," Christine said to the pizza guy as she leaned up to get her slice. Andy looked at her, nearly spellbound, as she turned back around to him and said the impossible.

"You going anywhere to eat your slices? Do you want to grab a bench somewhere?"

"Uh, sure," he replied, not sure to what to attribute his good fortune.

"Great, I'll go out and scope one out around the corner, meet me out there?"

"Yeah, be right out!" he said, wondering if it was as obvious on the outside that his blush had deepened. And off she went through the door with Andy's eyes trailing her out and across the front window back to campus.

This was not the way Andy expected his life to go, generally speaking. The most beautiful, and yes, desirable woman he had yet encountered in his college experience was supposed to be a distant object of beauty tinged with anxiety. She wasn't supposed to be so easy to approach and she certainly wasn't supposed to be the one who approached him and asked him to sit down and eat pizza! His heart raced as he considered his good luck and feared it would soon run out.

Within minutes he had his slices, freshly warmed from the oven then sandwiched between flimsy paper plates that acted as much to absorb the spare grease from the cheese as to serve as an actual plate. He bolted out the door and down to the corner, hoping that she hadn't thought better of her invitation and disappeared. Rounding the corner and looking down the street, there she was, occupying a bench on the opposite sidewalk. The Spring sun was pouring down over her and as he looked her way, he nearly had to pinch himself that such a lovely image was looking back at him, waving him over to sit down by her.

"What a day, huh?" she said, motioning for him to sit down.

"Yeah," he said, aware how dull his responses generally had been but unable to construct anything more intelligent than that.

They chewed their slices in silence for a bit before she spoke.

"So you're working for Gordon."

"Yeah, I mean, I was already, I mean, I TA'd your class."

"Oh, that's why you were there, handing me my papers back," she started, gently mocking him, "I thought you were just really interested in early American history," she finished, laughing.

"Right," he chuckled along with her. "I am that, too."

"So I figured. I can't say I'm as into it, but if you're going to study American history, Gordon's about as good as it gets, I imagine"

"He is."

"He's super religious, too, right?"

"He is."

"How does that work?" she asked, then with one glance his way, seemed to realize that she had inadvertently walked right into the thick of it. "I mean, not that it's a big deal, I just wondered if, you know, that was something…"

She trailed off and he was happy to chew on a big bite of pepperoni-laden crust while he figured his response. Finally, he swallowed hard and jumped right into it.

"No, that's exactly why I'm here with Gordon this summer. I don't really need to take classes this term, I just really want to work with him on some of his projects."

"Some of his religious projects?"

"Yeah, he's doing some cool things."

"Like?"

"Like, compiling the journals of the early religious freedom advocates of Rhode Island, you know that was one of the first colonies founded without allegiance to a specific religious sect."

"I do remember that from his class."

"Oh, right, sorry," he apologized with his body, backing down a bit from his excited description. "Of course you remembered that, you did get an A in his class."

She smiled and now it was her turn to blush.

"I guess I should've realized that you would know my grade. Did you get to read my papers, too?"

"I didn't read all the papers, just a few of them, Gordon grades them all himself, I just record them and get them organized to be handed back." His answer deliberately avoided the question itself. How would he explain that even if he didn't have to grade her papers, he had chosen to read them all, because, well, she was that intriguing to him? And to be fair, her papers were good, so that even if he knew he was reading them to get closer to her without having to actually maintain a conversation with her, he persisted in reading them because they were good.

With one more bite her slice of pizza was gone and she was wrapping up her napkin and plate to go.

"This was fun, Andy, I'm off to the library to copy some articles before my next class, I'll see you around."

"Yeah, thanks. I hope so."

She slipped her backpack over one shoulder and looked back down at him, searchingly.

"Are you a religious guy, too?"

Was this a test? He didn't know, but didn't try to outthink it.

"Yeah, yeah I am."

She smiled. "That's cool. Alright, see you around."

Was it a test? If so, did he pass? He chewed some more pepperoni and wondered.

Definitely a highlight of the entire semester, he thought.

Chapter 3

Finding the *Guinness Book of World Records* in the bookstore wasn't so hard. But thumbing through it to find the record for holding your breath was pretty frustrating, navigating the miniscule low-contrast type of the big paperback. Eventually he paged to the right place and discovered that in 1959, Robert Foster had held his breath for thirteen minutes, forty-two seconds, a time made possible by hyperventilating with pure oxygen before beginning the feat. Definitely a long time. Almost subconsciously Andy started to hold his breath right there in the bookstore while he took out his journal. By the time he got his journal open and was writing the answer down, he already felt a desire for air and was surprised to see how little time he could go without breathing.

Closing and reshelving the book, Andy glanced at his watch, waiting for the second hand to cross over the twelve o'clock position. Then he took a deep breath and held it, watching the seconds and stepping his way down to the ground floor of the bookstore and then out the door. By the time he turned right down Comm Ave and had made it nearly to the corner, he could hardly suppress his lungs' need to breathe. Stopping on the corner, he managed to go a few more seconds before he finally gave in, gasping for air and answering the pressuring need he felt inside his chest.

He looked at his watch. He had held his breath for one minute and ten seconds, a tiny fraction of the time the world record holder had managed.

Crossing the street, he managed to keep at bay the thoughts that were trying to invade his mind. If one minute is that hard – if nearly fourteen minutes is a world record – then how could someone possibly stay inside a whale for three days without air? This was exactly the kind of thought that Andy had hoped not to have to wrestle with. For all this time he had blithely gone along with the Jonah story, never once stopping to consider the logistics of it all – did Jonah have air, how long did he go without it, all of that stuff. But now, thanks to Tentworthy's insistence that Jonah's story was a test for all Christians, Andy couldn't stop coming back to all the little bits of the story most likely to cause him to lose the very faith that just twenty-four hours ago he believed he had!

What had Gordon said?

If you want it to be easy to believe, you have come to the wrong place.

Is it wrong to want it to be easy to believe? Andy found himself resenting Gordon just a bit for pushing some of these thoughts forward in his mind when all along he would have preferred it if Gordon had taken the questions away from him. Why couldn't he just focus on the parts that are easy to believe? Wasn't every story a mix of obvious truth and some convenient abbreviating to help make the story make sense or save space or something? Gordon could have just waved his hand and said, "Focus on the parts that seem right and leave the rest a bit vague."

Yet that was exactly what Gordon could not do. That's why he was such a distinguished scholar. He refused to leave things a bit vague. He followed the truth no matter where it led him.

And that is what Andy wanted, too. Or he wished he could want.

He briskly made his way down the side streets to the library to conclude the final task assigned to him before his upcoming 4pm appointment with the professor. The bookstore had provided access to the book of world records easy enough, but while there he had realized that to use a basic dictionary like those so readily available at the bookstore to define the word *literal* was not sufficient to the task. Because Gordon had not asked him to merely define the word but to find the literal meaning of the word itself. This represented a challenge, Andy knew, because Gordon never misplaced a word in an assignment, even one scribbled on a piece of yellow notepad paper.

The reference section of the library was more than willing to assist him in his task. His own work for Gordon, first as a student in the class and then as an assistant, had made him intimately familiar with the reference section. His love for and familiarity with the reference section as a result of his many fruitful searches through its tomes was something he took a bit of smug, albeit quiet, pride in. Where other students moaned at the thought of having to trudge to the library in a Boston snow to look up a historical definition of a term or to find the source of a well-worn quotation, Andy had come to relish the chance to pour over the thick and intimidating books in search of nuggets of knowledge. Because he knew that these books held the kinds of truths that were so important, other smart people in history had compiled them into handy guides. Seen this way, the dreaded reference section was actually a shortcut to knowledge, a way to quickly know what mattered and what did not.

Though it wasn't something he would likely admit to in social settings, Andy had previously spent an hour engrossed in a completely surprising volume called *The Oxford Dictionary of English Etymology*. The book's sole purpose was to describe the origins behind words and phrases, identifying, where possible, the first use of a particular term. Where other dictionaries like the Webster might explain the root of a word, saying that the word *chef* came from the French word for *chief*, which a head chef was in the kitchen, the Oxford would quote the earliest references for the word in its various senses.

He knew right where the book was on the shelf and proceeded to thumb through it, thinking ahead of himself. Literal, the root is certainly Latin, he surmised, for no other reason than that it didn't sound Germanic or Greek or anything else. But he wasn't a linguistics expert, he didn't know what *lit* meant other than it also showed up in words like literature and litany, though he wasn't sure they were necessarily related.

Literal: late 14c., "taking words in their natural meaning," originally referring to Scripture and opposed to mystical or allegorical. From lit(t)eralis, "of or belonging to letters or writing."

It made immediate sense to him. Literal and letter had the same root. A little digging into the word letter led him to a clearer sense of it. Letter came from *littera*, which is Latin for letter of the alphabet.

He jotted this down but didn't know immediately what to make of it. So the word *literal* came from the word for letter. That didn't seem to help. Where he had hoped that Gordon was leading him down a path where he could somehow excuse Jonah's story for its unbelievable elements, Gordon's questions seemed to be leading him in exactly the opposite direction. How was this helping?

He was tired by this point, he found himself looking over the definitions in the books and rereading them, not because this actually helped him understand them, but because his lack of sleep the night before was muddying his mind. For a brief moment he grew drowsy and put his head down in the open book.

A second later he sprung awake in response to a hand on his shoulder. His neck had a crick in it and his forehead felt dented from the pressure of the book against the open pages of the Oxford. Someone was nudging him and he shook the sleepiness from his eyes to glance at his watch, only then realizing that it wasn't a second later, but twenty minutes later. The nudge on his shoulder, he realized, came from the reference librarian who finally spoke.

"Time to wake up," she intoned, quietly.

"Sorry," he began, trying to act like he had it all together, but was aware that any attempt to explain himself would make him seem even more pathetic.

"It's not like you're the first person to fall asleep in the library," she said gently, but not without chiding.

He laughed politely while frantically collecting his things. He was already late for his appointment with Professor Gordon and swiftly calculated the time it would take to get out of the library and down the block to Gordon's office.

By the time he arrived, he was huffing a bit, very aware of how fatigued he was after a night of no sleep and a day of puzzlement.

"There you are," Gordon greeted him.

"Sorry, I, uh, I fell asleep." Andy left off the part about doing so in the library. He figured what bits of his reputation he could save he would.

"No trouble," the professor said, putting the papers and books in front of him to one side and swiveling his chair toward Andy. "What do you have for me?"

Andy pulled out his notebook where he had copied down the three tasks and the answers he had collected by way of response. He handed it to Gordon and looked at the man's face expectantly as he scrutinized the marks on the page. Some nodding and murmuring occurred, Andy couldn't tell if it was a general murmur of approval or not, but he tried not to read too much into the professor's countenance.

Finally, the man said, "Well, what do you think?"

Andy blinked. He didn't know what to think. Wasn't Gordon the professor? Wasn't he the one who was supposed to do the thinking and the evaluating?

"I dunno," he finally offered up, not sure what else to say.

Still tired, but eager to move forward, he finally ventured into the silence left by Gordon's refusal to answer his own question.

"First, I learned that the word *whale* doesn't appear anywhere in the book of Jonah."

"Good. So what?"

"It means that I've learned the story wrong my whole life."

"Wrong?"

"I guess so. I mean, I've always thought it was a whale and it never occurred to me to doubt that."

"Why?"

"Because," he was reaching now, not sure where Gordon was trying to take him, "It never occurred to me that the story as I heard it wasn't true."

"Do you mean that the story wasn't true or the way it was told to you wasn't true?"

Andy pondered this, wanting to say, *what's the difference?* But he held back from jumping to that question, assuming that there was something in there for him to understand. Then he saw it.

"If the story was told to me in a way that wasn't true doesn't mean the story isn't true." He blurted this out, a bit excited that even in his fatigued state he could parse things like this.

"Whose fault is it that the way it was told to you wasn't completely true?"

This one really stopped Andy, he wasn't sure what it meant.

"Whose fault? I guess, no, I don't know that anyone was at fault, really. In fact, the idea that a whale might be responsible is a pretty logical conclusion, so I don't think that it's necessarily wrong to guess that a whale may have been involved."

"Whales aren't fishes, you know."

"What?" Now Andy was annoyed because Gordon seemed to be taunting him. He shook his head and maintained what he hoped was a calm demeanor.

"Whales aren't fishes, not technically. They're mammals."

"True, but I don't see what difference it makes. I mean I don't really know what word was originally employed in the Hebrew, but I doubt they had as fine of distinctions as that in their understanding of marine life," Andy was now going on the offensive and though it felt uppity of him, it felt a relief to have some convictions to share.

"Meaning?"

"Meaning that whatever animal it was that swallowed Jonah, the word he used in his native language to describe it might have included whales and large fishes both. Or he might have used a word that is more akin to sea monster or something." Even as Andy was thinking this through out loud he realized he was talking himself more and more into possible doubt.

"Exactly!" Gordon beamed at him.

Andy sighed, uncertain why this gave Gordon such pleasure. Sensing his dispirited state, Gordon now stepped in to illuminate matters.

"We're playing a game of telephone here, Andy, and we're playing it across thousands of years, multiple languages, and many retellings. Just as the well-meaning people who taught your boyhood Sunday School classes chose to make the story easier to visualize by telling you it was a whale – and to be sure most of them probably didn't realize the word whale wasn't even scriptural – they were only the most recent ones to add their own grease to this sticky axle."

Andy thought this over and realized that he had said more in his previous comment than even he realized.

"You mean," he began to piece it apart, "that from the moment the story was first told, it was subject to this same process, this game of telephone as you called it."

"Almost certainly."

Andy sat back in his chair across from Gordon, raising his hands to his face to rub his reddened eyes. Where just hours ago he was sitting on a bench contemplating his good fortune to share a slice of pizza with a girl who was a heavenly revelation in her own way, now he was back in the pit of potential despair, wishing for a direct revelation by heavenly messenger. Frustrated, he sighed once again, placing his hands down at his sides and exclaimed.

"How does that help me?"

Gordon regarded him for a moment, calculating some things, then responded.

"It doesn't yet."

"Good, I'm glad we agree on that."

"Andy," Gordon said, with less amusement in his voice than had been on display throughout the conversation thus far, "I know this is hard. I believe it's supposed to be. And if it helps you to hear it, I will tell you again that the story of Jonah is true. But to understand what that means, you're going to have to puzzle out some more things than this. Rome wasn't built in a day as they say and the souls of men are certainly no different."

Though he felt chastised, Andy also felt genuinely reassured. Gordon was really going to help him, he was sure of that. Perhaps Gordon was the only one who could.

"Let's pick up where we left off with the other two assignments I gave you. What did you learn?"

"I learned that barring some miracle, a man can't hold his breath for even fourteen minutes."

"Barring some miracle?"

It was his own words repeated back to him as a sincere question, one that Andy hadn't realized he was even asking. One that he didn't have an answer for.

"Then what."

"I learned that the word *literal* is pretty much what it seems. A letter-by-letter or word-by-word meaning of something."

Looking over the notebook, Gordon pulled something out of Andy's notes. "It says here that the word was used in reference to scripture as early as the fourteenth century. What does that mean?"

"It means that people have been suggesting that scripture should be interpreted literally for a long, long time."

"At least six hundred years or so."

"Right, a long time."

"But how long has Christianity existed?"

"Nearly two thousand years," Andy replied, but then remembered who he was talking to, knowing that Gordon sided with those who considered the Old Testament a lengthy but crucial prelude to the arrival of Christ, which at least to his eyes made Christianity as old as Adam.

"So Jonah wasn't a Christian?"

"Not in the technical sense, no."

"So why do we Christians care if his story is true, can't we just set it to one side?"

Gordon was baiting him.

"No, we can't. Because Christians believe in the Bible, all of it." Then regurgitating what Gordon himself taught about the foundations of American Christianity each semester, Andy continued. "Because we believe that God put the Bible on the earth to prepare us to know about, welcome, and receive His Son."

"Do you believe that, Andy?"

Without hesitation, despite the previous night's sleep-depriving doubts, Andy answered.

"Yes."

"Do you realize what you've just said?"

To be honest, he did not, so he said as much.

"No."

"You've just asserted that the Bible has a purpose."

"Of course it does."

"Good, can you restate it for me? Better yet, as you restate it, write it down at the bottom of your notes here," Gordon instructed, handing the notepad back to his student.

Andy started to write what he had just said, not sure if it fulfilled the assignment but moving ahead anyway. He spoke it aloud as he wrote.

"The Bible prepares us to know about, welcome, and receive Jesus Christ."

Gordon seemed pleased, leaning back in his chair for a moment, smiling.

"I think we're going to make progress here," he said finally. "To summarize, we've found out that the word *whale* is nowhere in the account of Jonah. Which means that we can't be sure of the words recorded in the Bible itself. Yet at the same time we have a centuries-old tradition that the Bible should be read literally. Sandwiched in between there we have the fact that a man can't hold his breath for even an hour much less three days. Confused yet?"

Andy nodded. He didn't feel the need to admit to it out loud.

"Good, because we have some time."

"Time until what?"

"Time before you have to stand before the altar of God and affirm your belief in him. Before you have to participate in communion, to take the blood and body of Christ as an act of faith rather than merely an act of obedience."

The words sank deep into Andy's mind. These were heavy words and they landed with appropriately heavy feeling, almost dread. Six days didn't seem like enough time to heal all of the wounds in his faith. He voiced this fear.

"Six days until Sunday? That's not a lot of time."

"You're right, it's not a lot of time, but I don't want you to think of it as six days. Instead, think of it as six ways."

"Six ways to Sunday. That doesn't help."

"Six ways to Sunday indeed. I like that, actually. Let's use that," Gordon continued, suddenly enthused. "Since today is running to an end and you are obviously exhausted, I'm going to give you a jump on Way One. You've already done the legwork for it, but tonight, before you go to bed, before you say your prayers, I want you to do something."

Gordon leaned forward, retrieving his own notepad and began to write. His strokes were quick and determined. Andy waited patiently, glad he didn't have to do much more thinking because the ability to think was escaping him after what felt like a long and bruising day.

Finally, Gordon tore the sheet off from his notepad and handed it to Andy.

"This is your assignment to complete day one – no, Way One. Come see me tomorrow morning, 9am, and we can get started on Way Two. Yes, I very much like this Six Ways concept."

Andy glanced at the sheet, but did not study it, he knew there would be time for that. He bundled up his things and started out the door but not before Gordon stopped him.

"Andy?"

"Yes?"

"How many ways does Jesus love you?"

It was a more evangelical statement than Andy was used to hearing from the faithful yet reserved professor.

"I don't know, I assume a lot?"

Gordon just nodded and turned back to the work at his desk.

~

How many ways does Jesus love me?

Andy contemplated this question all the way home, though his tired mind muddled his thoughts as he walked. He'd never thought to ask the question before. Sure, if someone had asked, "How *much* does Jesus love you?" the easy answer was a lot. But how *many* ways was a different way to think of it and his brain couldn't quite get a handle on it.

One thing his brain did get quite a handle on was the memory of Christine. Her white shorts lingered on his mind. She really was beautiful in all the ways a young college boy would care to think of. He tried to brush that thought away, for several very good reasons. One, she was clearly out of his league. Two, well, he was a Christian boy and believed it was right to bridle one's passions. Which was very hard to do in this school surrounded by people who thought chastity was just the name of a belt from the middle ages.

He turned his mind to the task ahead of him, taking out the paper where Gordon had written the assignment. He slowed his steps so he could read it.

Way One: Accept that you don't know what you don't know. Then go further and admit that you don't even know what you thought you knew. God will not put new wine into old, unclean bottles. Clear your mind of prior assumptions, open yourself to whatever God wants you to know.

Andy prepared a little dinner of chicken noodle soup, Saltines, and an orange Crush. He pulled the paper out again and thought it through. He had been given three assignments. The first one, find the word *whale*, had been easy enough to understand. It isn't there, but Andy assumed it had been. In Way One, Gordon had written *admit that you don't know what you thought you knew* and he had also said *clear your mind of prior assumptions.* Okay, so the word *whale* is vague, the scripture might mean something else. He was good with that, at least as good as he could be for now.

The second task, finding out how long someone could hold their breath, that was a bigger problem. That one didn't seem as easy to overlook. Because whether a whale or a fish or a sea serpent, there's really no way someone can survive in the belly of something for that long. He wanted to put it aside, but knew it would just keep him up all night because it was the kind of dilemma that had started this whole chain of doubt.

He looked back over Way One to see if he could connect it to the breath problem. *Clear your mind of prior assumptions.* There weren't any prior assumptions to deal with in this case, holding your breath was holding your breath, except–

Wait a minute! If the scripture didn't say anything about whales, it didn't say anything about holding one's breath, either. This realization struck him with the force of revelation. The scripture never said that Jonah held his breath. It never said that Jonah even had to hold his breath. This was part of what Gordon was driving at, Andy was certain. *Accept that you don't know what you don't know.* If God never said it, then don't assume it, and certainly don't try to hold God responsible for your assumptions. Putting yourself constantly on the edge of doubt if God doesn't satisfy your assumptions is like asking God to be something other than He is.

It's like asking God to be your version of Him for your own comfort.

Andy found himself energized by this idea, even though it was a chastisement of his own thought processes. But it was also liberating. The story offered challenges enough as it was. It was unnecessarily complicating to add assumptions of our own and then insist that God address those, too.

Humility. Andy realized it was the very definition of humility. Not the kind of self-doubt or kneeling down before an altar to show who is boss, but true humility. Accepting one's inferiority to God, not because it makes Him happy, but because it puts us in a position where He can finally teach us.

God will not put new wine into old, unclean bottles. Of course, Andy could finally see it clearly, why Gordon acted so smugly confident that things weren't as bad as they seemed. Because things have to get bad – at least if you think being humble is a bad thing, which people almost always do – before they can get better.

Andy took out his journal and copied down Way One from the note Gordon gave him. Then added his own thoughts.

Humility! God can use scripture to strip away all our worldly assumptions, to put us in a place where we admit we know nothing. Only then can we be guided to the truth.

Truth. There was that word again. The truth was supposed to make Andy free and only from this position of greater humility – or lesser pride, Andy wasn't sure which was the better way to describe it – could Andy see that the search for truth itself was already freeing him, freeing him from assumptions that were holding him down, putting scales over his eyes, and making him vulnerable to doubt.

By adding all of these assumptions, Andy had actually deviated from the letters in the scripture, the *literal* facts of the scripture. That realization was the icing on the cake and liberated something inside of him and suddenly he felt exhausted, spent, but in a way that induced a peace and sense of trust he desperately needed.

Within minutes of this breakthrough feeling, his head was on his pillow and Andy thought no more about whales, holding his breath, or decoding letters. He slept freely for the first time in two days.

Chapter 4

The morning light was not unwelcome. Andy glanced at his watch, he hadn't even taken the time to remove it last night. It was already eight o'clock and Andy was relieved that the relative peace he had achieved the night before had not disappeared as he slept.

Was he cured? It wasn't really the question that he expected to ask himself. Gordon had said there would be several days of work, but here he was already feeling better about the little crisis of faith he had experienced not even two days ago.

Was he cured? Maybe that wasn't so bad a question after all. Perhaps he could meet with Gordon this morning and assure him that they could get back to their regular research. After all, Gordon had important work to do that didn't involve leading Andy through tales of whales, Ninevites, and so forth.

He kept up in this vein through most of his morning routine, he even found himself whistling in the shower. He breezed through the cafeteria, grabbing some pieces of toast and a glass of juice, with a silly smile on his face. And why not? It was a beautiful summer morning in historic Boston town. Maybe he'd even go for a walk down Newbury street this afternoon after his history class.

He even arrived early at Gordon's office, tapping softly on the slightly ajar door before leaning in to push on the door. He heard Gordon's voice, however, and leaned in to make sure he wasn't interrupting anything before proceeding through the door. But what he heard gave him pause.

"Kevin, I don't know that I can help you with this." Gordon's tone was serious, even a tad despairing. Knowing it was bad manners, Andy kept listening to the silence of Gordon's side of the conversation.

"This is out of my realm – don't misunderstand me, it's fascinating and maybe it's wonderful, but it's also…very…unorthodox. To say the least." Gordon leaned back on his wooden chair, Andy could tell because he heard the familiar creak of the chair, one that signaled the professor was pondering something intently.

"I understand, yes, I know that you need something, I just don't know what it is. Let me, well first let me pray for you, right away. And then, well, we'll see what else I can offer as I consider it some more."

Then Gordon moved to end the conversation, causing Andy to lean back away from the door, suddenly guilty of eavesdropping on a man he knew would expect better of him. Stepping back slowly, he listened for any overt sounds of movement that signaled Gordon was ready to be interrupted. Still, it remained quiet and Andy found himself unsure. Trying to pretend he hadn't been there all along, he stepped back up to the door and knocked, loudly, as if he didn't feel he should be trying to soften his arrival.

No response through the door. Generally, Gordon had an open-door policy when the door was, well, open, as it was now, if only slightly. So Andy knocked again and started to step through the door.

"Professor Gor—" was all he managed before he saw the man kneeling beside his desk, evidently in prayer. Now he really felt ashamed, stepping slowly back through the door and quietly attempting to close it.

"Andy?" it was the professor's voice, and if he was annoyed at having been interrupted, his voice didn't betray it. "Come on in, I'm finished."

Seeing another man pray was not a shameful thing, and Andy knew Gordon had no qualms with his faith in general, and certainly not in dealing with Andy. But something sensitive had transpired in that conversation and Andy didn't want to accidentally reveal that he knew something was going on. He put on his brightest face, the one he'd been wearing anyway just minutes ago due to his newfound feelings of relief, and stepped back through the door.

"Sorry about that, Professor, I was a little early and I guess I didn't realize it."

Gordon stood behind his desk, hands drawn to his hips, sleeves pushed up a bit. It was evident he had been in his office for some time already, even though it was only nine in the morning. His greying hair was unkempt and he looked at Andy with a mix of fatherly feeling and slight distraction.

"No trouble at all, Andy, no trouble at all. Please, come in, sit down, let's see," he shuffled some things on his desk and sat back down, indicating all the while with his hand the invitation for Andy to take a seat in one of the chairs opposite him. "Now where were we? Oh, yes, tell me first how you're feeling today?"

Andy knew his face had answered that question already but Gordon hadn't noticed yet. Certainly something was troubling the man. All the more reason for Andy to relieve Gordon of the burden of worrying about Andy's Jonah problem, if it could even be called that.

"I'm great, I got a lot of sleep last night, I feel a lot better. In fact, I feel like we may not even need to meet on this today."

Gordon, still moving stacks of papers around, paused at this, looked at Andy. His face was somewhat surprised and perhaps somewhat skeptical. Andy offered back a broad grin, thinking it argued his case without further comment needed.

"That's certainly good news," he returned, then kept looking at Andy, expectantly.

"Yeah, it's a huge relief, you know I even think maybe we don't have to spend our research time on this problem anymore."

Now it was Gordon's turn to smile. He seemed visibly relieved, at least for a moment as he returned to thumbing through stacks of papers.

"You think so, huh? Well, my friend, it is far too late for that!" Laying hold of a legal pad with some notes on it, Gordon retrieved it and reviewed his own writing as he spoke. "You don't know what you've initiated here. Your dilemma has given me a good excuse to put some ideas down on paper." He fanned through the legal pad, pulling sheet after sheet up to reveal a fluid cursive manuscript, many pages long.

"You wrote all that since last night?" Andy asked, his incredulous tone matching the rising of his eyebrows as he spoke.

"Yes, mostly since I got here at five this morning, actually," he said, pausing briefly to take in a particular page, where he promptly pulled out his pen and made a few edits. "There, much better," he muttered and for a moment Andy felt he was eavesdropping again.

"I got about thirty pages in so far, thanks to our conversation yesterday. But I don't know how it ends, not yet, anyway." He looked up at Andy. "That's where you come in."

"Me?"

"Yes, we have to see this through to the end so I know how to finish what I've started." Gordon looked at his watch, "Goodness, it's already late and I need a doughnut. Let's go to Dunkins for a coffee and a cruller."

He stood, feeling for his wallet, which was not in his pocket, then he felt around the stacks of papers on his desk until he found it.

He gestured to the door, "Shall we?"

~

Whatever the serious conversation had been about, it didn't seem to hang over Gordon's head as they walked down Comm Ave to the doughnut shop to pick up a cruller each and let Gordon grab a coffee. Even though Gordon was a very controlled and disciplined man, Andy had learned that he did have a weakness for pastries, especially during times of stress or fatigue. Andy tried to push aside any questions about what stress Gordon might be feeling connected to a phone call that he shouldn't have heard in the first place. Instead, he assumed it was his situation that was causing the anxiety and aimed to relieve that problem.

"Like I was saying, I'm doing much better, so I'm not sure we—"

"I'm going to ask you a question, Andy, before you say anything more."

They paused for a streetcar to pass and then they crossed the street, walking into the older streets and buildings of campus. Nibbling on his cruller, Gordon paused at a bench, dappled by sunlight successfully penetrating the canopy of leaves, and motioned for the two of them to sit.

"You say you're feeling better and that's great. I believe you and I'm happy for you. Before you say anything else, I want to ask you this question." He looked at Andy intently, and without blinking, asked, "What are you feeling better about? You're doing better than yesterday, certainly. But are you actually better off than you were before you went to Tentworthy's lecture Sunday night or have you simply reverted back to what you felt before Tentworthy made you feel uncomfortable?"

It was a classic Gordon question where Andy knew that there was much more to it than one heard at first listen. He wanted to say he was 'better' and in fact that's exactly what he had said. And now Gordon was challenging his choice of words because to be better suggested something more than recovered. True, he had recovered from his setback, but he hadn't advanced at all. He puzzled all this out in his own head, chewing a bite of his pastry, then admitted in a low voice.

"I guess better isn't exactly right."

Gordon regarded him, finished the last quarter of his cruller with a single bite, then lifted his hand to his chin with a ponderous look. "Pity, really, I would be thrilled if you had already made it to the other end of this, then you could just fill me in and I could complete my notes on the situation." Then with a broad smile, he brought it back, "But I'm not surprised. If it were that simple to get to truth, truth wouldn't be worth much."

"From faith, through doubt, to truth," Andy nearly whispered, as if remembering it from a long time past. Then louder, "Professor, that's what you're talking about, isn't it? Just going back to faith from doubt, stepping back to that place of relative innocence, it's not the same, is it?"

Gordon answered by leaning forward, extending his hand from his chin where he had been resting it, gesturing to suggest Andy take it a bit further.

Andy picked up the hint. "Faith isn't as good as truth?"

Gordon leaned back and furrowed his brow a bit. Clearly Andy had gone the wrong way.

"Of course not," Andy talked his way back, "Faith is always good, it's just not, it's just—" now he was a bit lost where just seconds ago he thought he was grasping it.

"It's just not complete," Gordon offered.

"Because only the truth shall set you free," Andy added, looking at Gordon for approval. The grin on Gordon's face suggested he had recovered. They paused, Andy wasn't sure if there was more to say, but Gordon didn't gesture for him to continue so he stopped.

Seemingly satisfied, Gordon stepped in. "Andy, the truth is marvelous, certainly. But it doesn't set you free in itself. It's really the act of finding your way to the truth that sets you free. Because once you do it once, you can do it over and over. Until the perfect day."

The perfect day. The phrase seemed familiar to Andy but he couldn't pin it down at first. In all of this his head was starting to swim again. He felt a bit lost compared to the buoyant feeling he'd had in the first hour he had been awake. But it was a good kind of lost, a lost that came with a resolve to find his way. Not *back* to the path, but to a *higher* path. That really would set him free. He counted himself lucky that a man like Gordon would take this time to bring him along. And not be content to merely affirm his faith but to do so much more. Catching up to Gordon, he popped the last bite of his cruller in his mouth, chewed, and resolved himself to tackle the next assignment, whatever it may be.

"You have your notebook?" Gordon asked.

Andy reached for his backpack to show that he did.

"Good. First, remind me what you learned yesterday."

"Humility." The word tumbled out almost immediately. It was the most succinct way to describe what Andy had learned and he had evidently internalized it because he didn't need to think of it before it speaking it.

Gordon's smile broadened. "Good. Very good, in fact. You took what I sent you home with and then clarified it in your mind. You followed the chain that linked the application back up to the broader concept. We *are* making progress!"

"So where do I go from here?" Andy asked, notepad out and pencil in hand.

"Right into the brink!" Gordon roused with evident enthusiasm. "Today your task is simple. I want you to just believe!" He chuckled as he said this, which was a bit surprising for Andy since it wasn't clear he had made a joke. Pencil in hand, he waited for his next instruction.

Evidently aware that he was acting a bit odd, Gordon stifled his chuckle and explained. "I want you to take God at his word. You already know what the word literal means, I want you to scour the account of Jonah and the whale – or, as you now know, the fish – and believe in every single word."

Andy still hadn't written anything down because he wasn't sure there was anything to do. Not yet anyway.

"Can you do that?"

"Do what?"

"Believe. Believe in the story *as is!*"

Andy was perplexed. It was his discomfort believing the story as is that had gotten him into this situation in the first place. How was he supposed to just command himself to believe it? And would that really be the truth that would set him free?

"I'm not sure I get it," he said, suppressing the slight annoyance he now felt, an annoyance that was in sharp contrast with the way he felt just an hour ago, a fact that annoyed him even further.

"No, I doubt you do, not yet. But let's hope you will." This was the first condescending thing Gordon had said to him yet and it intensified his annoyance. He held it in.

"But what do I *do?*" he asked, somewhat exasperatedly, pointing to his paper with his pencil to indicate it was still blank.

"Make notes," Gordon continued in a lighthearted tone. "Make notes on everything in the story that would require a miracle in order to be true."

Andy slowly scribbled that down. *Believe in the story as is. Note the miracles needed.* Suddenly the assignment was taking on a more interesting flavor. He was starting to see how this could be both a challenge and a useful process.

He clarified, "So when you say, 'Believe in the story as is,' you are saying, that I should assume that the story is true, and when the story bumps up against the facts—"

"Facts?" Gordon interrupted him.

He paused, understood he'd already forgotten the lesson from Way One, and began again.

"When the story bumps up against the *assumptions* I have made about the story, about the way the world works," then he caught himself, "about the way *I assumed* the world works, then I should believe that God could just insert a miracle."

"Hmm, insert. Good choice of word there, I'm going to remember that one and put it in my notes, with your permission of course."

"Of course," Andy replied, suddenly flattered.

"Then once you've identified where the miracles need to be *inserted*," Gordon said, emphasizing this last word, "describe what the miracle might look like."

Andy made further notes, but now was less certain. He looked up. "What it might look like?"

"Sure, as in, what would God have to do to make this story literally true?"

It seemed a tad irreverent to Andy to put it that way, and unusual for Gordon to speak so instrumentally about God and His purposes, but it did make immediate sense and for that bit of clarity Andy was grateful.

"In other words, believe in this story *as is*," Gordon pronounced in a deliberate tone. "Call that Way Two if you want."

Way Two, Andy wrote back at the top of his notepad.

Gordon stood. "All right, time to get back to some other matters. I won't be free until 4pm so come by my office then?"

And with that, they parted.

~

Sitting back in the library, Andy began to read.

Now the word of the Lord came unto Jonah the son of Amittai, saying, Arise, go to Nineveh, that great city, and cry against it; for their wickedness is come up before me.

He hadn't thought of it this way before, but technically, there was already a miracle here. For the Lord to speak to Jonah and give him a message, it had to be done in some fashion that Andy hadn't personally experienced.

He pulled out his notepad and wrote:

Miracle 1 – The Lord communicates directly to Jonah.

That's the miracle, he understood, but Gordon had asked him to describe what that might look like. Referring back to the verse, he made some quick decisions about what this meant. It didn't say the Lord appeared to Jonah, but only that His word came to him. Andy thought that through and figured that it could happen in any number of ways, but if he was supposed to believe in the story *as is* then he had to conclude that some words came to Jonah from outside himself without any other being present or at least visible. There were only a few ways that could happen. He either heard an audible voice or he heard a voice inside his mind. Or, Andy figured, it was possible that some words were written down in front of him, on an object or in the air. But that seemed really unlikely given that the verse didn't say anything about words or an object. So Andy wrote:

Jonah hears the voice of the Lord, either out loud or in his mind. Somehow, God can speak to us, either by causing the air to vibrate with the frequencies of speech or by causing our minds to perceive sound.

Andy didn't prefer one explanation over the other. Either was surely miraculous. Yet completely easy to believe. If God created everything, then he has power to command it to move, including the air. If God created us, then he certainly has power to manipulate the mechanisms inside our bodies – our nerve endings or our brain waves, Andy didn't know which – in order to speak to us directly. How he did it was uncertain. But that, Andy realized immediately, was why Way Two was focused on just believing. He had to believe that God could accomplish this miracle. And as he reflected on it, he found that he had no trouble whatsoever believing that God could, in fact, make this miracle happen.

Here was a miracle and an affirmation of Andy's belief, already in the first verse. Not the miracle he imagined he was looking for – that would come later in the form of a fish. But this was a miracle without which the other miracles wouldn't have happened at all. Miracle leading to miracle leading to miracle.

He continued to read, finding his second miracle just a few verses later.

> But Jonah rose up to flee unto Tarshish from the presence of the Lord, and went down to Joppa; and he found a ship going to Tarshish: so he paid the fare thereof, and went down into it, to go with them unto Tarshish from the presence of the Lord.

> But the Lord sent out a great wind into the sea, and there was a mighty tempest in the sea, so that the ship was like to be broken.

He wrote:

Miracle 2 – The Lord causes a mighty tempest.

Even as he wrote this he understood that a storm didn't have to be a miracle. Unlike with miracle number one, this miracle – a stormy sea – happened all the time and could be explained directly by meteorologists. Except that in this case the storm was clearly sent by the Lord to accomplish His purposes. The Lord "sent out a great wind." Andy considered that for a moment, and then keeping with what he had written before, he added an explanation of what that miracle might look like:

Somehow the Lord caused a wind to blow with such force that it created a significant sea storm. This would involve moving the elements — the wind, the water — and doing so in a targeted fashion, aiming for Jonah's ship.

He was getting the hang of the exercise, he thought, seeing here once again that if God could create the world he could certainly manage its affairs. True, Andy didn't see that God was behind every wind, every wave, and every tempest, but certainly, if one was reading this story and choosing to believe, God was behind this one. That's what made it a miracle, just as it was when Jesus calmed the seas when he and his disciples were adrift in a storm. But Andy wasn't sure about *how* Jesus did this. Did he communicate with some kind of primal spirit inside the air molecules? The thought left him a bit uncertain. And a bit uncomfortable to just fill in the gaps with the word miracle. But Gordon had told him to believe and that's what he was willing to do.

Then the mariners were afraid, and cried every man unto his god, and cast forth the wares that were in the ship into the sea, to lighten it of them. But Jonah was gone down into the sides of the ship; and he lay, and was fast asleep.

So the shipmaster came to him, and said unto him, What meanest thou, O sleeper? arise, call upon thy God, if so be that God will think upon us, that we perish not.

And they said every one to his fellow, Come, and let us cast lots, that we may know for whose cause this evil is upon us. So they cast lots, and the lot fell upon Jonah.

Now Andy was a bit concerned. Is this a miracle? The text doesn't insist that it is, but it seemed to be more than coincidence that the lot would fall upon Jonah. So Andy wrote:

Miracle 3 — The Lord makes the lot fall upon Jonah.

Somehow the Lord directed the lot — whether it was dice or a drawing of straws or something similar — to fall upon Jonah.

That's as simple as making the dice fall a certain way if it was a cast lot, Andy figured. If God can control the wind he can move the dice. If it was the drawing of straws or something like that, then it would require directing the hand of the other people to avoid drawing the short straw. That was a bit different. Suddenly, God was making people behave in a particular way, even though God seems to be a respecter of people's free will. Of course, He could do it if He wanted, He was God. Maybe God just changed the length of the straw in the moment to ensure that Jonah's lot grew smaller as he chose it. That was also a possibility. The more Andy thought about it, the more he realized that calling something a miracle wasn't just a way to fill in the gaps of knowledge, but it was also a way to point out a range of possibilities, a range that Andy was willing to accept on faith. That's what belief was.

This was a bit freeing. He had already accumulated a slight defensiveness about so-called miracles, even before Jerry questioned Tentworthy's Jonah dilemma. Because it seemed convenient to say, "it was just a miracle!" as a way to blindly avoid the tough questions of faith. But just as he was learning from Gordon that there were Six Ways to Sunday, there were six ways to understand every miracle, with each one being miraculous in its own right. But you wouldn't see that if you weren't first willing to believe.

And maybe that's what Gordon wanted him to know from this exercise, Andy realized. Maybe there's a difference between hiding from the complexities of God by calling everything a miracle and embracing the potential power of God by being willing to believe in the miracles He achieves, via whatever means He achieves them.

Andy wasn't sure this was the intended lesson or even a lesson at all, but there was something there. If he could just choose to believe.

Then said they unto him, Tell us, we pray thee, for whose cause this evil is upon us; What is thine occupation? and whence comest thou? what is thy country? and of what people art thou?

And he said unto them, I am an Hebrew; and I fear the Lord, the God of heaven, which hath made the sea and the dry land.

It wasn't a miracle, at least not in the traditional sense of the word because miracles usually refer to things that God does. But it was remarkable that Jonah, knowing full well he was opposing the Lord by sailing directly away from Nineveh, would dare tell the men his real identity. So if not a miracle, what was it? Jonah had to know that the consequences of him telling the truth would be dire. Yet he did so anyway. God didn't cause his mouth to move – the text doesn't ask us to see it that way – yet the Lord did give the opportunity for Jonah to step up and account for his own decisions by causing the prior miracles. That was a miracle on its own. Who knew that a handful of verses of just one chapter could yield so many miracles and so many important lessons for life? Even though he was loving the process, Andy was getting a bit concerned that perhaps he was reaching too far or seeing things that weren't there to be seen. But he figured the worst thing that could happen was that Gordon would chuckle at him for overreaching. Taking up his pencil, he wrote:

Miracle 4 – Jonah chooses to tell the truth.

By putting Jonah in a series of significant circumstances, the Lord gives Jonah an opportunity to acknowledge his mistakes and begin to make amends.

He stopped, looked back at what he had written, feeling like it was a bit wordy, like the real point was buried. Then, in a flash, he realized there was a much better way to say what needed to be said.

Jonah repented.

A kind of energy moved through Andy at this thought. It wasn't just the simplicity of the words but the ultimate power of what he had recognized. Miracle four really was a miracle after all, because of all the winds God could blow and all the lots God could influence, this miracle was the greatest of all. When one of God's children free-willingly repents and turns back to God, and God accepts him, that is the greatest miracle of all.

A powerful peace settled upon him. There was something achingly profound here and Andy knew it. In all his searching for the secrets of faith someone like Gordon surely had accumulated, Andy had never had such a clear and direct manifestation of God's ultimate purpose in his life.

Repentance. Forgiveness.

Eyes brimming, Andy set his pencil down and just pondered this moment. *May I never forget this feeling*, he prayed in his heart.

Then were the men exceedingly afraid, and said unto him, Why hast thou done this? For the men knew that he fled from the presence of the Lord, because he had told them.

Then said they unto him, What shall we do unto thee, that the sea may be calm unto us? for the sea wrought, and was tempestuous.

And he said unto them, Take me up, and cast me forth into the sea; so shall the sea be calm unto you: for I know that for my sake this great tempest is upon you.

Nevertheless the men rowed hard to bring it to the land; but they could not: for the sea wrought, and was tempestuous against them.

Miracle? Andy couldn't be sure. Again, he felt that the word miracle applied to things God did, not the things that people did. And even Jonah's miracle – that he repented – is only a miracle because God forgives him. But still there was something special about the way these people responded to their situation. The fact that they fought against the storm wasn't so much an act of rebellion against God but an attempt to clear themselves of wrong doing. They didn't want to harm Jonah and they didn't want to be held guilty for aiding his escape. It seems clear that their intent was to simply return Jonah to the beginning, get him back to where he came from and thus be free of it all. Yet the storm – or the Lord – would not permit their efforts.

No, this wasn't a miracle, but it was a lesson about who was ultimately in charge. Still, despite God demonstrating His power, He would not simply take all the men and the ship down with Jonah. He made their journey difficult, but He did not take away their choice.

Wherefore they cried unto the Lord, and said, We beseech thee, O Lord, we beseech thee, let us not perish for this man's life, and lay not upon us innocent blood: for thou, O Lord, hast done as it pleased thee.

So they took up Jonah, and cast him forth into the sea: and the sea ceased from her raging.

Miracle 5 – The storm stopped.

This one was easy to believe in. If God could cause a tempest He could certainly end one. He began to write.

God again directed the wind and the water around Jonah's ship.

This captured the miracle itself and was easy to believe in. But he found himself wanting to write more. Wanting to *believe* more. Because the miracle was the easy part. The real miracle was that God spared the men on the ship, that He pardoned their unwitting participation in Jonah's flight. If Jonah's miracle was repentance, God sparing these men was also a miracle and believing in it was much easier – and had a much more profound effect on Andy's mind – than simply trusting that God could cause and end a storm at will. In fact, Andy found himself grateful that God had caused the storm in the first place, just so that the redemption from its effects could be so beautiful.

This was a bit of a dilemma, to Andy's mind. Here he was trying to work his way out of a crisis of faith, a profoundly negative storm of his own, believing that he needed to find shelter from this storm of doubt. Yet the most beautiful miracles of the Jonah story so far were Jonah's repentance and God's willingness to spare the men despite their mistakes. Those miracles, ironically, were much easier to believe in than causing the wind to blow or the long straw to grow short or any of those things. Yet those were precisely the miracles that everyone would have avoided if God had never caused the storm to blow.

The storms of life put us in the position where we are most prepared for the true miracles of repentance and forgiveness.

I didn't want this storm, Andy thought, wondering if he should write that down. *Yet even in these few days it has caused more miracles than I have experienced in my life so far.*

Then the men feared the Lord exceedingly, and offered a sacrifice unto the Lord, and made vows.

Andy's heart was swelling with a warmth that enlivened him. He knew the feeling that motivated the men. He feared the Lord in the same way – not in a cowering or simpering way, but in a humble, believing way.

Miracle 6 – The men make a commitment to follow the Lord.

That was what was happening here. They offered a sacrifice, the Old Testament way to make a covenant and a promise with the Lord.

They made vows. Andy wished for a way to make a vow. In some ways these people had it easy. When they felt this strong pull to fall into line with God's will, they knew just were to go. To the temple to offer a sacrifice. Andy had a sense that his baptism, something he had chosen to do at twelve years of age, was his sign of the same thing. But he felt such a strong connection to the miracles of the story of Jonah that he wanted to find another vow to make. It was a miracle in his own heart that he knew was happening in that very moment.

Andy's eyes grew wet as he let the surge of – was it love? – course through him, like blood pumping to every cell in his body. And he knew. He believed.

Miracle of miracles – I believe.

Tears came to him now, freely.

Now the Lord had prepared a great fish to swallow up Jonah. And Jonah was in the belly of the fish three days and three nights

A gentle laugh bubbled up inside Andy. Here it was, the pivotal moment, the big challenge to his faith. Where Jonah was swallowed by what Andy always thought was a whale. This was the miracle that everyone talked about, it was the miracle he had spent the last few days sweating over, it was the miracle that had caused Andy to stumble. And here, looking at it now, after he had spent these long, thoughtful moments awestruck by the power of the other miracles in the chapter, this single, solitary verse at the end of the chapter seemed, well, downright inconsequential.

The soft flow of tears from his eyes stopped. He closed them and pondered what he was feeling now, trying to formulate the perfect words.

Miracle 7 – God sends some kind of fish to pick up Jonah. The fish was big enough to envelop Jonah and God directed it to swallow him then hold him for three days. Miraculously, Jonah survives the ordeal.

It was such an easy miracle to believe in when it came right down to it. Certainly, if God can control the wind, the water, the casting of the lot, then God can control an animal, aquatic or not. And perhaps an additional miracle was needed, the "preparation" of a special fish.

Maybe it was of a species that doesn't otherwise exist or perhaps it was a giant among its kind. Whatever it was, God prepared it, sent it, and it accomplished its mission.

It was not only simple to believe this story as is, it was a joy to do so. Because once you've embraced the biggest miracle of all – that God loves His children and has prepared a way for them to repent and be forgiven – accepting the minor details of a prophet and his fish was very simple.

He put his pencil down and reflected on how he felt. There was a warmth in his body, in his soul. A sweetness he didn't want to forget. He knew the source of it.

He believed.

Chapter 5

It was time for lunch and Andy knew what that meant. He would find any possible excuse to go to the pizza joint where he had run across Christine the day before. He knew it was too much to hope for, that she would be there, that she would want to keep the conversation going, that, well, anything. He knew he should just be glad for what he had and not push for more.

But off he went, hopeful beyond hope. The day was clouding up, not uncommon in Boston this time of year, though it always came as a surprise mostly because you can't see the clouds coming from very far off the way you could in Andy's Midwestern hometown. Too many trees between you and the horizon. A breeze carried him along down the street from his apartment to the pizza joint where he kept his head down as he stepped through the door. If she was there, he would be embarrassed at how obvious his intentions were, if she was not there, then he would be embarrassed at how much he had hoped for such a small thing. His face flushed warm just thinking of his mini catch-22, embarrassed if she does, embarrassed if she doesn't. There was no way to win. Wasn't that often the case with pretty girls?

Waiting in line to order his slices, the delicious smell of oily mozzarella wafting over the air, Andy finally dared to lift his eyes and scan the line of people ahead of him. There was a blond head, which momentarily caught his attention. But it was attached to a much older woman and Andy soon found himself desperately craning his neck to find Christine elsewhere in the place. She was not there.

Not realizing he was leaning forward on the balls of his feet, he settled back on his heels and shook his head a bit, unaware of the chuckle coming from his own mouth. He had halfway convinced himself that it was better this way, better that the memory of his brief lunch with her remain just that, when of a sudden, he felt a light hand on his back.

Startled, he turned and there she was, beaming brightly up at him, eyebrows raised in what seemed genuine happiness at seeing him.

"Hey there!" came her lovely voice, every bit as enchanting as he had remembered it.

"Oh, hey, hi." His words did not come easily, though for a moment he couldn't even muster the nervousness he knew he should feel at having seen her. He couldn't because her presence was so welcome.

"I thought that was you," she started, filling the small space between them with words. He turned to her and watched as her hand withdrew from around his shoulder and found himself wishing desperately he had a good reason for her to put it back.

"You come here often, I guess?" he managed and even though it sounded like a pickup line, it was sincere.

"Yeah, definitely. I'm here for the red pepper flakes." Her face broke into a full grin that nearly stopped Andy's heart.

"I'll have to try those." And again the words failed him. He had spent the whole walk over imagining how awkward it would be to run into her here. He realized he should have been rehearsing what he would say if he actually encountered her.

The line moved forward and Andy was grateful for the foot-shuffling time.

"So, you and Professor Gordon working today?"

"Um? Yeah, we are, or we were, early this morning." He didn't quite know how to explain that working, at least this week, didn't really feel like work. At least not the work you got paid for.

"What are you working on?"

Of course, that was the question she would ask, and it was obviously the thing he should have answered with in the first place. Why was this conversation-with-a-beautiful-woman thing so hard?

"It's sorta, I don't know, kind of unusual." Shifting his mind away from acute awareness of her delightful presence, Andy began to access the part of his mind that had spent the morning on Way Two. Looking back at her, he finally answered clearly with one bold word, "Miracles."

"Miracles?"

"Yeah," he started to stutter again, not sure how much to reveal about his crisis of faith or lack thereof. He headed in the direction of avoiding all of that. "Gordon wants me to identify miracles in specific stories in scripture."

"Like Moses, that sort of stuff?"

"Yeah, only I'm focusing right now on Jonah."

"Oh, the whale guy."

From behind him, Andy heard, "What can I get ya?" and he turned to realize he was next in line.

"Um, two pepperoni slices and a lime soda," he replied, then pulled out the change from his pocket to pay.

"Funny you should say that," he continued over his shoulder to Christine, "because, well, did you know that the word whale never once appears in the book of Jonah?"

"Oh? Interesting."

He paid, waited for her to order and reflected on her ho-hum response. Was he about to bore her with his studies? Maybe she wasn't religious and didn't care. But seeing that he didn't know what else to say to her while they waited for their slices, he continued.

"Yeah, it never says Jonah was swallowed by a whale. Instead, it says a fish did it."

"That's some fish," came her answer, and her smile was still there, but Andy couldn't tell if it was less interested than before.

"I know, a huge fish. That's one miracle, I guess. That there was even a fish that big in the neighborhood."

Her look was still genuine and even genuinely interested, but Andy didn't know if she was interested in the topic, in him, or in her slices of pizza warming in the oven. He changed the subject.

"What about you, what have you been doing this morning?"

"Definitely sleeping in!" she returned, her smile coming back to life. "I managed to load all of my summer classes up on Monday, Wednesday and Friday. That way I can use Tuesday and Thursday to do all of my homework." Then, realizing what she just said, she added, "Or not, as in the case of today." At this she laughed and when her eyes tightened, he saw in her look a kind of happiness that he wanted in his life.

Was he falling in love with her?

"But I'm supposed to be working on a chemistry lab right now. I mean, I should be. But I opted to come get lunch instead."

Yes, he was definitely falling in love with her.

Their slices were ready and as they came out on their oily paper plates, he grabbed the red pepper shaker and shook flakes out onto his pizza. More came out than he expected, so he tried to act cool about it.

"Woah, hold your horses there, I told you I liked them, not that I recommended you take a bath in them," she teased him.

"It's all right, I can handle hot stuff," he said, realizing how it sounded, then blushed.

"Oh, you can, can you?" she looked back at him with a wry grin.

Most definitely falling in love with her.

Pulling away from the counter she preempted the question he was hoping to ask.

"Where should we eat today?"

We? The word was like manna from heaven.

"I don't know. Same place?"

"No, we have to strike out into new adventures!" Her grin was positively enchanting.

"Okay, well, we could always go over to the esplanade," he offered, shrugging his shoulders as he leaned into the door to leave the pizza place.

"It's a date, then," she chirped. And Andy suddenly grew warm in the face. Followed by growing warmth in his hand as he inattentively turned the pizza in his grip, allowing the grease to drip out of the paper plate onto his hand. A date? And he was starting it by wiping grease off of his hands with his only napkin.

They walked down Deerfield toward the bridge to the water under a darkening sky, Andy not sure exactly how to make this "date" go smoothly. The part of him that couldn't believe what was happening to him was giving way to a part of him that was certain he would say the wrong thing, or otherwise blow it. Luckily for him, she directed the conversation.

"You didn't finish," she started, sipping her soda. "You were going to tell me more about the whale, or fish, or whatever miracle."

"Oh, yeah."

"Why does Gordon want you to find miracles?"

It was complicated and Andy didn't know how deep to go. He wasn't going to share his crisis of faith with her, he decided, but he also didn't want to make stuff up. So he just kept to the facts.

"I think in this case, he's making a point that maybe the miracles we think of aren't really the miracles that matter at all. Take the fish thing, for example. When you hear Jonah, what do you think?"

"Whale."

"Right."

"Which isn't even right, it's a fish. If that distinction matters."

"Also right. But did you know that the whole bit with the fish doesn't even come into play until the final verse of the first chapter of Jonah?"

"No."

"Me, neither. And in the story, it's a real minor event, by the time you get to it, there have already been six or so other miracles."

"None as big as the fish, though, right?"

"Big in size, maybe not, but big in importance, yeah, I think that's what Gordon's trying to get me to see."

"Like what?"

Andy realized he was talking to Christine as if she were a believer, which he wasn't sure of. Obviously she wasn't a stranger to scripture. And she was asking, so it was only natural to answer her question. But how could he convey the power of what he felt that morning in a way that captured what he experienced but didn't also put him out on a limb with her. A limb he wasn't sure he was ready to jump on lest it break.

He fell silent for a moment as they walked the pedestrian bridge over the rushing cars below. The wind off the water was blowing with more force and spring clouds were really gathering. Between the wind and the traffic it was too loud to talk, giving him more than a few moments to consider his words. *Repentance. Forgiveness. That's the miracle.* Those were the words he wanted to say and even thinking them with such conviction started to recall a glimmering memory of the powerful feelings he had while he was studying. But his tongue failed him.

"I don't know, like, I don't know," were the first words that escaped his mouth after they had crossed and were walking down onto the grass. *Good*, he thought, *very impressive*. "Like forgiveness. It's not as big as a fish, but…maybe it's a bigger deal."

"Okay," she nodded, indicating with her paper plate a nearby bench where they could sit and finally dig in to their food. "I like that."

She liked that. He liked that she liked that. He was in serious trouble here.

In that instant he felt a few drops of rain. He had been so captivated by the pleasant company that he'd barely registered the impending rain.

"Oh, no," she responded as she felt the same drops on her face. "Nothing's worse than wet pizza!" she declared, cramming the triangle point of her slice into her mouth, desperate to get it while the getting was still good. He joined her with enthusiasm, and they laughed as they chewed, a drop of cheese oil running down her chin.

The rain picked up steadily, though it never switched into torrent mode, so they still sat there for a moment, beneath the edge of a tree, eating. Then, as the rain intensified and the tree above them served to filter fewer and fewer drops, they instinctively stood up and sought cover closer to the trunk of the tree. She was done with her slice and sipping her soda, her hair falling a bit to the sides of her face, wet as it was. The unkemptness of her now-wet hair combined with the gusto of her laughter at their turn of affairs made her even more attractive. Sexy, even. He crammed the last half of his second slice into his mouth at once.

"I definitely won the pizza eating contest," she teased.

"Okay, little Miss One-slice," he teased her back, mouth still gnawing on his last bites. "I won't deny the facts of the statement, but I think it's obvious that in a fair fight," he paused, swallowed, "I would have prevailed."

That's when the rain really let loose. They were maybe fifty feet from the bridge back to campus, and Andy was eyeing it not so he could run back across the bridge but because it looked like the best actual cover for the rain. The tree they were standing under wasn't doing much good anymore.

"Let's make a run for it," he said, stepping ahead of her, but turning back to her.

She reached out her hand and he took it. With it, she took what was left of his heart. Propelled by his numb happiness, he turned into the rain and pulled her along, her squealing at the rain and him soaring inside.

They reached the cover of the pedestrian bridge and tucked themselves under the stairwell to wait out the rain. She was laughing, he was panting, his heart quickened by more than just the brief run.

She slowly released his hand and had he known how much he would later reflect on her letting go he might have paid more attention in the moment. Did she want to let go? Did he make it clear that she didn't have to? Oh, this falling for someone business was really getting to him.

As they leaned against the wall, safe from the rain, he took a good look at her. Her hair was good and wet now and the effect it had was positively alluring. As if everything about her didn't already have that effect on him.

Smiling back, she said, "A question for you, Mr. Miracle."

"Shoot." *Anything for you.*

"Be honest."

"Okay."

"Did you go to the pizza place today hoping to find me?"

He couldn't have lied if he wanted to. His face betrayed him, his smile gave him away, and his rising blush would have seemed a beacon from a mile away.

"Yes."

She paused, smiled more deeply, more intently.

"I thought so," she said. "Me, too."

And then she kissed him.

Chapter 6

Best day of my life.

There weren't many more words to describe it. Andy momentarily debated whether to explain why in the pages of his journal. It seemed incautious to do so. After all, in twenty years from now, if he were reading these words and Christine was still in his life, then he wouldn't need to say what happened because it would have become part of his life story. And, if she wasn't in his life, he knew that he would be embarrassed at the memory of how happy that kiss had made him.

She kissed me.

It was detail enough, he decided, and set his pencil down, adding all the words in his mind that he wouldn't put on the page.

True, it wasn't a big kiss. And technically, it wasn't even a kiss, in that it was more of a cheek kiss, with a little bit of lip in there. That detail made it all the more tantalizing, though, because it left him to wonder if she had deliberately crossed lips with him, or if it had been an accident. And if an accident, was it a happy one? Was she glad of it?

Suddenly he realized that maybe it was an invitation. Or possibly a test? Had she hoped he would seize the moment and kiss her back with cinematic force?

Now he was a mess of second guesses and equivocations. He tried to convince himself there was no need for that. The kiss had been a simple lean-in, head-back, up-on-toes reach for his cheek. Maybe she missed, maybe she meant to miss, but when she pulled back she was smiling. He knew he certainly was. And then the moment was over.

His walk home had been full of wonder and astonishment. How did...? What the...? Questions didn't even have the chance to fully form in his mind, he was so surprised at his good fortune.

Once inside his dorm he went to the bathroom and looked at himself in the mirror. Reddish hair, decently tall, thin to the point of distraction. What would interest her in him? He looked again, hazel eyes, skin a little freckly but not alarmingly so, short hair not fancy but not a mess either. He looked harder. Maybe he wasn't as average as he assumed, maybe this is what attractive looked like?

He shook his head. No, he was no Tom Cruise, that was obvious. He was more the sidekick look, like Goose to Cruise's Maverick in *Top Gun*. And Christine was even cuter than Kelly McGillis. So why was she interested in him?

There were feelings of insecurity rising in him over the question. All attempts to put the insecurity and the larger question of what she saw in him aside failed miserably. There was this fact: She had kissed him. And the warm memory of her kiss still contrasted with the coolness of the sudden rain. It was an unexpected, if glorious, outcome and he could not explain it to himself. But that didn't stop him from obsessing over it.

He took a deep breath and looked in the mirror again, with this simple thought in mind: *What does she see in me and how do I make sure she sees a lot of it?*

~

He barely paid attention in his afternoon class. It was post-Civil War America, not his favorite period, but one he was well versed in, so he didn't need to pay full attention. Which was good given his distracted state. When class finally ended it was time to return to Gordon's office. Thoughts of Christine still percolating in his head, Andy returned to his notes from before as he walked through a cloudy but no longer raining campus. Seven miracles, each of them pointing to the same great miracle. God loved His children.

For God so loved the world, that he gave his only begotten son, that whosoever believeth in him should not perish, but have everlasting life. John 3:16.

That scripture came to mind unbidden, yet it was the perfect explanation for everything. It tied each of the seven miracles together in a single reference.

Arriving at Gordon's office door, Andy didn't see the envelope taped to it until he had already knocked on the closed door. The envelope had *Andy* written on it in pencil. Pulling it off the door, Andy felt a weight shift in it as he turned around to inspect it.

Sliding his finger in an opening, he pulled the envelope open, careful not to let the object inside slip out. There was a single sheet of paper and, as Andy suspected, a key.

Andy, I had to make an unexpected trip to New York. But not before I left you some notes on my desk in my office. Keep the key until I return.

Unexpected was an understatement since just a handful of hours ago the two of them had agreed to meet here to review Way Two. Slipping the key into the door handle, Andy cautiously cracked open the door and seeing nothing here but the afternoon light casting a glow across the room, he entered.

Closing the door behind him, Andy glanced over at the desk where he saw a legal pad filled with notes. Eager to see what lay in store, he set his own things down and pulled up Gordon's chair. The leather of the chair added an aroma of authority to the room, just sitting in it made Andy feel smarter, reassuring him that he was closer to an answer than he might otherwise feel.

Dear Andy,

My apologies to you that I had to leave unexpectedly. Perhaps someday I will have the opportunity to discuss the reason for my journey with you. It is quite unorthodox in some ways but very promising in others. But we have other matters to discuss, you and I. The first being your experience with believing, or Way Two, as we will call it. I have given this some thought myself and were we together I would want to ask you various questions such as, "What did you learn about yourself

from believing?" or "What did you learn about God from believing?" And finally,
"What did you learn about Jonah's fish?"

We will have that conversation at some point, but until then, I want to prepare
you for Way Three, as I will not be here tomorrow morning for us to begin that
process. But I would like you to do some things tonight in preparation for Way
Three. And then I will plan to call my office tomorrow morning at 9am where I
hope I will find you ready for the introduction of Way Three.

Your assignment tonight is to watch Star Trek *on channel five at 6pm. If I*
remember right you do not have a television in your dorm – something I commend
you for, by the way – and so you may need to find one in a dorm common room or
elsewhere. Pardon the unusual nature of the request, I believe you will see better
tomorrow when we chat at nine o'clock.

Until then,
Professor Gordon

This was the second time in the same day that Gordon had used
the word unorthodox. And given his relative interest in preserving
tradition – the man read the King James version of the Bible, for
heaven's sake – it was interesting that he seemed to be using the word
without judgment. This intrigued Andy, especially in light of the very
unorthodox assignment he had just received.

Star Trek?

It's not that Andy didn't know the show, he had grown up
watching reruns of the classic show in middle school. It was a bit of a
sad routine, he now realized, but he had come home from school,
grabbed a snack each day and watched first *The Brady Bunch* and then
Star Trek. He had probably seen every episode of both shows multiple
times over.

But that Gordon knew about *Star Trek* seemed at odds with his
generally respectable manner. Andy smiled a bit, realizing he had
judged the man for reasons that weren't entirely clear. There wasn't
anything wrong with the show, nothing unchristian or inappropriate,
nothing like that. It's just that, well, the show seemed kind of frivolous.
Certainly unGordonly, Andy thought, happy with the word he had just

coined, a word he realized he wouldn't get to use ever in his life since no one else would understand it.

Grabbing his own bag and retrieving his journal, Andy turned his attention to the three questions Gordon suggested they would someday have the chance to discuss. He wrote them down, leaving space between each one, and then went back to add some notes.

What did you learn about yourself from believing?

That I am a believer. I enjoy it. Especially when I know that the thing I am believing is so good. Taking away the questions that I have and trusting in the ultimate power of God strengthens me.

He looked back at this and realized it was possible to take it more than the way it felt to him. Because to him it felt good, powerful, and elegant. But on the other hand, the way he just described it, believing could be seen as just an excuse for not wrestling with the questions. If it was merely this kind of blind faith, then it would eventually land Andy back in the problem that had caused this week of study in the first place. Because at some point he would find something that he couldn't believe at face value and would be driven to doubt again. But Gordon had said Andy would not merely sidestep or avoid doubt but would come through it. Maybe that's why believing was Way Two. There were still four more to go, four ways in which he would, he presumed, come back to the tricky questions and prepare to know the truth.

What did you learn about God from believing?

I learned that God has a bigger purpose behind the scriptures than just entertaining or even overawing us with stories. Miracles are miracles, yes, but they serve a purpose, and that purpose is love.

This was important. And something that Andy couldn't seem to find an adequate way to resolve in his mind. Because to see God's grander purposes so clearly, he had to submit to the possibility that God was doing things that he didn't understand. Miracles. That's why Way One had been humility: only in the lee of humility could Andy find the stillness that allowed God's purposes to come through so plainly.

What did you learn about Jonah's fish?

That the fish is the least important part of the story, as far as God's purposes are concerned. Yes, God has power to do what He determines is best. But more importantly, God will seek after us, God will not let us fail if we are willing to entrust ourselves to His care and keeping. Even if that means passing three days in the belly of a fish.

Here he was, coming back around to the power of the idea of being swallowed by a fish. That was supposedly the most difficult part of the story, or at least the one that had triggered the sleepless night of doubts at the outset of the week. And yet here Andy was seeing just how beautiful this fish tale really was, even if it was, as he had just written, the least important part of the story. The fish, yes, was unimportant, but God's purposes, as shown through the fish, that was masterful.

Andy leaned back in the professor's chair and felt a sense of purpose himself. This is what life is about, he thought. Seeking God, yes. But, more important, having the distinct confidence that God can actually be found.

~

Finding a place to watch *Star Trek* was not going to be as easy as that. Gordon remembered right – Andy didn't have a TV in his dorm room. It wasn't a virtue, it was really a function of poverty. From his jobs as a kid he'd saved up money for basic expenses and his parents were helping with tuition. But if it weren't for the scholarship he'd gotten from the university's history department, he wouldn't be here. Not bad for a Des Moines kid, he knew. But it meant that of money there wasn't much and a small TV for his private dorm room just seemed a good way to waste money and a bad way to waste time.

The TVs in the dorm's common rooms, on the other hand, were an option, except that they were typically dominated by sports especially with baseball season well underway. He could work his way up the floors in an attempt to find one that didn't have people in front of it. That might work.

Or he could call someone he knew might have one. A senior, say, who lived in an off-campus apartment like most grown up people (himself painfully excluded, he knew). One with whom he would love to spend some time. Oh, someone like Christine, for example.

Except how do you impress a girl by saying, in effect, "I still live in the dorms, I'm too poor to own a TV, and I want to come to your apartment for a romantic evening of *Star Trek?*"

All of this was true and should have inhibited him, but it did not. Instead, he was strangely excited to have a reason to call her. It was then that he did the one dishonest thing he had ever done in his role as a TA for Gordon: He looked up her grade sheet so he could find her phone number.

It couldn't be too dishonest, he reasoned. After all, she had kissed him. That was practically an invitation to call her right there. Or so he hoped.

~

"Hello?"

Pause. Andy had to reach for a dose of courage. "Hi, Christine?"

"Yes."

"Hey, it's Andy," he offered in neutral tones

"Oh, hi, Andy!" To his relief there was genuine delight in her voice.

"So I have an odd question," he began, uncertain how to proceed.

"Okay, shoot."

"Do you like *Star Trek?*"

~

It wasn't exactly the kind of question calculated to impress a young lady, but it was the most straightforward way to invite himself over to her place to watch TV, an odd request on the face of it and certainly unromantic for all the reasons he had rehearsed over and over.

But it had worked. She laughed when he asked, and said that while she wouldn't call herself a fan, she had watched enough re-runs with her brother growing up back in Virginia that she could at least hold her own in a conversation about the relative merits of Vulcan rationalism.

He arrived at her apartment just before six o'clock. She lived across the Masspike, over one of the bridges and in the alleys en route to Fenway. The apartment she shared with three other girls was cozy, which everything in Boston was of necessity. One of the girls, Melissa, was there listening to her Walkman and making herself some dinner in the kitchen. Christine had the TV on and had popped some microwave popcorn, the savory smell of which had filled the place, perhaps accounting for why the windows in the living room were open.

"Gordon wants you to watch *Star Trek*? As an assignment? Tell me more about this assignment," she said, plopping down on the sofa and motioning for him to sit with one hand while reaching for a handful of popcorn with the other.

"Assignment is probably an overstatement," Andy admitted. "He just told me to watch it and we would discuss tomorrow when he calls in."

"Calls in?"

"Yeah, he went to New York at the last minute, took the train down, he didn't explain why but there was some phone call, and, well, anyway that's not important."

"Important to him, at least," she countered, chewing some popcorn and smiling at him.

He realized that this was one of the things that he liked about her. One of many, true, but this one was unique. She was always paying extra attention to words, even the most casual expressions, and pointing out things about what he said that made him rethink what he was trying to say. Because it was true, the trip to New York was very important, in a way that Andy couldn't explain but certainly felt. But when he said it wasn't important, what he really meant was that he thought he was boring her with unnecessary details.

"Yes," he smiled, calmly. "Very important, I'd say," and he reached forward to the bowl of popcorn for some of his own. "Though I don't know exactly how. I kind of feel like that's my whole relationship with Professor Gordon. It feels like everything he says and does is important, but I am not sure I'm getting it."

"Hmmm. Classic case of hero worship."

"Hero worship?"

"Yeah, it happens all the time, or so my psych professors say. And it happens a lot on campus. When we learn these big, new ideas from adults who seem so wise, we have a tendency to confuse the source with the substance, and that causes us to fixate on the person rather than the ideas."

"Wow, that was pretty profound."

"I specialize in pretty profound."

All Andy heard was *pretty* because he would have gladly agreed if she had ended the sentence right there. She did specialize in pretty. But the fact that she also specialized in being profound made her a two-for-one special. Man, was he trapped in the idea of her. He wondered briefly whether there was a thing such as *Her Worship* because he had a good sense that he was doing it right now.

The show came on and their conversation shifted toward the show. As the drama unfolded, it was an episode that Andy knew very well, the original Khan episode, the one that later led to the movie, *Star Trek II: The Wrath of Khan*. Starring a younger Ricardo Montalban, long before he became Mr. Rourke on *Fantasy Island*. A kind of frightening episode about a man who is so much of a superior being that he can't be bothered to consider other, lesser humans as worthy of his respect or attention.

"Superman," Christine quipped as they watched the plot unfold, then explained. "It's the problematic German ideal of the *Ubermensch*," Andy noted her German pronunciation sounded smooth and, oddly, attractive. Or that was the *Her Worship* talking again. "Nietzsche. Zarathustra, all that."

And she silenced herself because the commercial that had afforded them the chat break was over and it was time to see the thrilling conclusion.

~

When they finished, it was seven o'clock and only then did he realize that he'd put himself in the very awkward situation of sitting on the sofa in the apartment of a girl he was very taken with. At that moment, he wanted nothing more than to just stay right there and never let go of that moment, a feeling he knew was foolish, but a feeling he didn't know how to push aside. He looked her way, wondering what should happen next.

"All right, Mr. Spock," she started, lifting herself from the sofa and carrying the empty popcorn bowl – had they really finished it all? The added weight in his stomach would have told him that they had if he'd paid it any attention.

"Or maybe you're not a Vulcan," she said, eying him up and down. "Definitely not a Kirk, and that is a compliment through and through, in case you were wondering," she tossed out a laugh and continued her way to the kitchen. "Bones? Scotty?"

Standing, following her hesitatingly, he responded with equal uncertainty, "I dunno. Maybe there's not a me on this show."

"No ship's chaplain?" she said, looking back from the kitchen over the bar.

He didn't know how to take that.

"No, er, not that."

"It's okay, you're the religion guy, that much I know."

Andy shuffled his feet and didn't know what to say.

"Come to think of it, have you ever noticed that there's no religion in Star Trek? I wonder why."

"I guess they think religion doesn't belong in the future," he said, with a bit of bitterness rising.

"Maybe they think people won't need it anymore." He couldn't tell if she was sad about this, or just observing. Still unsure of his place in her world, or her place in his, he didn't want to go deeper, even though he desperately wanted to ask, *what do you think?* Instead, he responded with a light humor that was comfortable enough.

"If I were dealing with rock monsters, mind-control plant spores, and Klingons, I think I'd want religion even more than I do now!"

Her smile broke the awkwardness. She closed the gap between them, placing her arm lightly around his waist and leaning back to one side to look up at him.

"Okay, the fun's over. I have a big test tomorrow and you, sir, are occupying my prime study time."

It was the gentlest shove off he'd ever received and if there were any sting to it at all, that was swallowed up by the feel of her hand touching the small of his back in a familiar way. With the same hand, she nudged him toward the door and he gladly let her.

"I'll let you get back to your priorities!" he said, and reached for the door, daring to say the one thing that he knew would gnaw at him all night otherwise. "Will I see you tomorrow?"

"You know what they say, 'Not if I see you first!'" Even this she delivered with such warmth that she could have told him he was lower than the sole of her shoe and he would have taken it as a term of endearment. "No, not for lunch you won't, that's when my test is, so think about me during lunch with fingers crossed."

How to explain to her that he would have absolutely no trouble thinking about her at lunch?

"I will do that. I'll eat a greasy pizza slice in honor of your test."

"And then?" she asked, eyebrows raised and leaning into him expectantly.

"And then?" was all he could reply.

"And then you'll meet me somewhere for dinner."

He was stunned. She was asking him out.

"I will? Of course, I will! I just don't know where."

"You'll figure that out, I hope, sometime before six o'clock tomorrow when you come pick me up. Or do you need to watch *Star Trek* again at that hour?"

Andy didn't actually know that, but he went with the thing he knew for sure, was that he certainly wanted to meet her for dinner.

"Klingons can wait. Picking up is exactly what I'll do. See you then."

"See you then," she said, eyes sparkling even as she pushed him, gently, out the door, releasing him and waving as the door closed between them.

Chapter 7

Andy awoke in the morning refreshed and with a song in his heart. Or a song in his mind. Unfortunately for him, it was the whistling theme to *The Andy Griffith Show*, a melody that plagued him all morning long, slipping from his mind to his actual lips more than a few times. That was fine in the shower or in his own dorm, but not in the street as he walked to Gordon's office. At one point he whistled that familiar tune so loudly that he was sure he was causing a scene, a hillbilly scene. He might as well have sung the theme song to *The Beverly Hillbillies*, that's how out of place he felt in the land of Harvard and MIT whistling an Andy Griffith tune.

Gordon's office was cool and refreshing, in contrast to the balmy day it was shaping up to be outside. Yesterday's rains had apparently brought in a new wave of warmth, the wet warmth of a Boston summer. He was glad for the air conditioning unit buzzing away in Gordon's window.

He had arrived just a few minutes before the hour when Gordon said he would call. This was really smart of Gordon, Andy realized, because calling in to his own office ensured that they'd be able to talk – Gordon's school-issued desk phone was a speaker phone, after all – and to do so privately.

The phone rang right on time.

"Hello? Professor Gordon's office."

"Andy."

"Yes, Professor."

"Good, glad you got the key, the note, all of it. Sorry again I had to leave you suddenly yesterday. I, uh, had some things to deal with down here in New York. I think I'll be coming home tomorrow morning, though, so don't think I've abandoned our project."

Andy felt reassured that Gordon had made it *our* project. Though he was certain Gordon didn't need it as much as he did.

"No problem," Andy started, "everything okay down there?"

"Here? Oh, yes, of course, nothing serious. Or not serious in, well, anyway, perhaps there will be time for that conversation one day." He drifted away for a minute and Andy in that moment took *one day* to mean a very distant day indeed.

Gordon asked for Andy's notes on the three questions he'd left the day before. Andy read his brief entries and for a moment they discussed the epiphanies Andy felt he had experienced. As he described them, they solidified in Andy's mind. Which was a surprise, he had originally thought that maybe his conclusions were too simple and would seem problematic or even naïve on later reflection.

The contrary was true. Finding in his core that he was a believer, knowing that God's purpose was love and that the stories He told were focused on revealing that love – well, the clarity of those insights only deepened as he described them to Gordon.

For his part, Gordon seemed pleased and after some minutes of back and forth, he then said, "Are you ready for Way Three then?"

"I think so," Andy replied, realizing that his hesitancy was unwarranted. "I know so."

"Good, because I'm going to ask you to go a completely different direction this time. You got my assignment."

"I did."

"And?"

"I was successful."

"Good, you found a common room or something like that?"

"Something like that." Something much, much better than that, actually, but Andy kept that bit to himself, even as his mouth refused to resist the smile that came over it.

"I bet you were wondering why *Star Trek*."

"The thought did occur to me."

"Did you come up with any ideas why?"

Andy didn't know whether to feign a sophistication that he did not have. That *Star Trek* was a metaphor for spirituality, that Kirk was a tragic figure, anything. Instead, he opted for bold honesty.

"No, none whatsoever."

"Good."

Good?

Gordon continued. "Here's what I like about *Star Trek*, besides the fact that the guy in the landing party with the red shirt always gets killed, have you ever noticed that?"

Andy laughed, despite trying to maintain his notion of Gordon as a very serious academic. If there was an element of Hero Worship in his relationship with Gordon – and since Christine had first said that, he had grown certain that there was – it wasn't even slightly undermined by the trivial observation Gordon had just shared.

"Anyway, what I like about *Star Trek* is that it tries to tell very human stories, mundane stories, really, about love, emotion, obedience, duty, all very regular things, but it tells those stories in a completely open and free setting."

That *Star Trek* was anything other than mindless fantasy had not occurred to Andy, but in Gordon's telling it suddenly took on new gravity.

"Believe it or not, I had you watch *Star Trek* purely to start your creativity flowing. Because Way Three is going to be very different from every other Way. Open the top center drawer of my desk."

Andy slid the small, wide drawer open to find pencils, some paperclips, and two pieces of legal paper folded in thirds.

"Okay, it's open."

"Good, now do you see yellow pieces of paper?"

"Yes."

"Take them out. They contain Way Three."

~

Way Three: Create

Andy looked at what he wrote at the top of his journal entry. Then he looked back at the first of the two pages Gordon had left him.

The writers of Star Trek *have the luxury of inventing whatever technology they need to accomplish their purposes. They can create any planet with whatever conditions they need. Though it purports to be a show based on a futuristic science, it's really just an exercise in expedient creativity. If you need to move a whole group of people from orbit to the surface of a new planet, you can invent a new technology that allows people to "beam" from one location to another.*

Your assignment as part of Way Three is to pull out the list of miracles you believed as part of Way Two, but this time, invent whatever explanation you need to make them true. If you need a technology, create it. If you need an explanation, invent it. Let your creativity be unfettered. But abide by these two rules: Nothing you invent should replace God's role in the story. Instead, it should just explain how God did it. And nothing you create should deprive the people of their freedom to choose.

Andy halted. He had reread this part several times and each time it still gave him pause. He didn't really want to engage in explaining how God did things. Weren't His ways not Andy's ways and all that? By trying to explain God's mysteries, wasn't he diminishing God in some way? But he trusted Gordon and was willing to accept that Gordon was working toward a more powerful outcome than just explaining God's miracles away. Even if it meant inventing ways to make Jonah's story real.

Andy had gone back to his dorm to work on Way Three, but the heat had accumulated in his room to the point where he realized he had to go somewhere else where his hard-earned tuition dollars were being turned into comfortable air conditioning. And so, with his Bible and his journal in hand, he trekked back out into the heat to find a nice empty study room in the library where he could create.

Along the way, he noted the hustle of the city. Campus was not particularly full, after all it was a summer term and the student body was likely only a fifth its normal size. But because Boston University was located in the middle of one of the country's largest cities campus always felt active. From the green line trains that cut right across the middle of campus to the foot traffic generated by Fenway Park just blocks away, Andy always enjoyed the energy here. Not just from other college students, either, but regular people. Hundreds of them, thousands of them.

And in this moment, walking down the street in his shorts and a sweat-stained t-shirt, he suddenly became aware of those people in a way that he hadn't experienced before. These many people on all sides of him, coming and going, with their own goals, their own hopes, their own decisions to make. He recognized that the week he was having, a week of doubts that he hoped, with Gordon's guidance, could become truth, was something he alone was experiencing. Perhaps the most important thing that had ever happened, would ever happen in his life, and he was having it alone. That all around him these hundreds, these thousands of people were missing this experience. This was a foggy realization. He didn't know what to make of it. The more he walked, the more people he saw coming and going on foot, others driving down the narrow streets, still others in the streetcars the locals called the "T." He realized that in this week he would possibly change his understanding of God, of life, of the purpose of this existence forever. And yet everyone else around him would remain unchanged.

This thought unsettled him. Was he better than they were? Was he happier than they were? He certainly didn't feel any of those things. But didn't he want this? Even if nobody else ever learned what he learned, wouldn't he still want the knowledge that he was gaining the way he wanted air and water?

Then, of a sudden, came this realization: If he did learn something that would change him forever, wouldn't he owe it to all of these people to try to share it with them?

Soon he was at the library and he pushed that thought, still only partly formed, to one side. Inside the library he found other heat refugees, some reading novels, some napping in the carrels along different hallways, but it was easy to find unoccupied reading rooms, especially on the higher floors. He browsed the stacks a little bit, running his fingers along the spines of books with titles like *Dedham*

Registry of Deeds, 1700-1726, and he was stunned for a moment to realize how long people had been in the Boston area, each of them wrestling with the questions of their existence, just as he was now doing, trying to reconcile themselves to God. Or not. What made him think he could do this successfully when many others had not? The question troubled him immediately.

Believe, he thought, almost letting the word slip from between his lips. Way Two was to believe and already the smallest questions about the process of believing were causing him doubts, only a day after feeling such a strong commitment to what he thought he believed.

To get himself back on track, he took out his list of miracles from Way Two and transferred them to a new page in his journal, this time summarizing the miracles for easy reference and further study. They were:

Miracle 1 – The Lord communicates directly to Jonah.

Miracle 2 – The Lord causes a mighty tempest.

Miracle 3 – The Lord makes the lot fall upon Jonah.

Miracle 4 – Jonah chooses to tell the truth.

Miracle 5 – The storm stopped.

Miracle 6 – The men make a commitment to follow the Lord.

Miracle 7 – God sends some kind of fish to pick up Jonah.

It was a daunting list, especially for Andy, who was a history major, not an English major. Or an aspiring screenwriter. Or any kind of creative anything. Still, he dove in.

Miracle 1 – The Lord communicates directly to Jonah.

This one seemed easy enough. Like everything else in this story, the details provided by scripture were scant. So he just had to make something up, right?

Now the word of the Lord came unto Jonah...

Under Way Two, he had been told to believe that this just happened. And that was pretty simple. Prophets had always received messages from God, whether through a burning bush; a finger carving words into stone tablets; or through the still, small voice Elijah reported. In most cases the communication happened without a medium of any kind, just like Jonah's case. The word of the Lord just came, like it did to Abraham, like it did to Moses, like it did to Samuel.

But how did it come? Andy's instinctive reaction was to begin speculating on how to answer the question correctly, to get the right answer. He knew this was wrong even as he did it. But he couldn't help it! His goal in life and certainly in this exercise was to find the truth and when speculating about scripture, his speculations were always directed toward the goal of finding out what had really happened. Way Two had been a challenge for him in that he was supposed to avoid trying to figure out what really happened and instead had to just accept what he read wholeheartedly. Already Andy could tell that Way Three would be much harder, not just because he would struggle with the act of creation itself, but because he had to open his mind to new ideas, impossible ones. Even if they weren't the correct ones.

Open his mind! That's what Gordon was going for. Andy understood that his conviction that God was real was a kind of mixed curse. He was certain about God's reality yet certainty of mind made him limited in mind. How could he develop a mind that could be both certain and unlimited at the same time? Not the kind of hippie unlimited that had seduced the generation before his, but a kind of unlimited that would enable him to see the grandeur of God while still seeing His practical presence. How can God be both things at the same time?

More importantly, how could Andy see God both ways – practical and transcendent – at the same time?

Create!

Absentmindedly, he began to doodle in the margin of his paper. A sweeping curved line became two, connected by a shorter curve, until he had a sketch of a leaf that had been stretched at one end into a teardrop-like shape. He lengthened the stretched edge a bit, then returned to the empty body of the shape where he drew an oval that nested inside the broader shape. Then he divided the oval with three lines that roughly trisected the oval into three rounded pie wedges.

Only slightly aware of what he was doing, he added modest shading to give the overall object a sense of weight. His sketching hand stopped and he looked at his creation anew. It wasn't a masterful sketch by any stretch, but it made sense. Without intending to, he had sketched the beginnings of one possible answer to the question posed by the simple phrase, "And the word of the Lord came unto Jonah."

Now fully swept away by the idea forming on the page in front of him, he added stroke after stroke, erasing occasionally, until the form become more concrete and the function solidified in his mind and on the page. Some minutes passed when he finally lifted his pencil and appraised his work. It was futuristic, no, not from the future, but from the past. Past-uristic? He smiled at this invented word because it conjured up the image of a misty, green field speckled with grazing cows. The image was silly but it was understandable given that his brain was trying to fit two conflicting thoughts together. How could the future fit in the past? In Andy's mind, Jonah was located in a past where there were only wooden ships, rough clothing, and poor hygiene. Yet the device he had just drawn was a communicator, not unlike something you would see on *Star Trek*, that could only happen in some future that was yet to come.

This sleek communicator would fit snugly in the palm of a hand, it would operate much the way the cheap Radio Shack walkie talkies of Andy's childhood did only with much more powerful range. A button to turn it on, a button to set the channel or frequency, and a button to talk.

Three buttons. Would there need to be a fourth? A listen button? Andy didn't want to redraw his creation, sketching wasn't really his thing and he felt lucky he'd even managed to produce something roughly identifiable on the first go. In the same impulse, he realized he didn't need a listen button.

The device would always be in listen mode.

Dots connected in Andy's mind. Of course God's method of communication would be continuous, uninterrupted, with small breaks for us to send questions the other way, but the default mode of the device would be listen mode. That's what made a prophet a prophet. The only thing he had to do was turn it on, and learn to tune into the right frequency.

This sleek little device perfectly encapsulated Jonah's obligations and still allowed him his freedom. He was a prophet – somehow, at some point, a prior prophet had given him the device. A listener? A revelator? A listenator? There had to be a catchy name for it even though Andy knew he was not the guy likely to come up with it.

Giving himself the freedom to roll with this idea for a bit – an idea that would be heretical to some, and maybe even to Andy if he gave himself time to think about it – what if a chief responsibility of a prophet was to receive the listenator from a prior prophet? That prior prophet would pass on the device, explain how it works, and basically say, "Do whatever this device tells you to." No, that wouldn't be right, because it's not the device that's talking. Instead, it would be something like, "God will use this device to give you instructions," – the instructioner? – "which you must follow. Your chief responsibility is to keep this instructioner turned on and properly tuned to God's frequency."

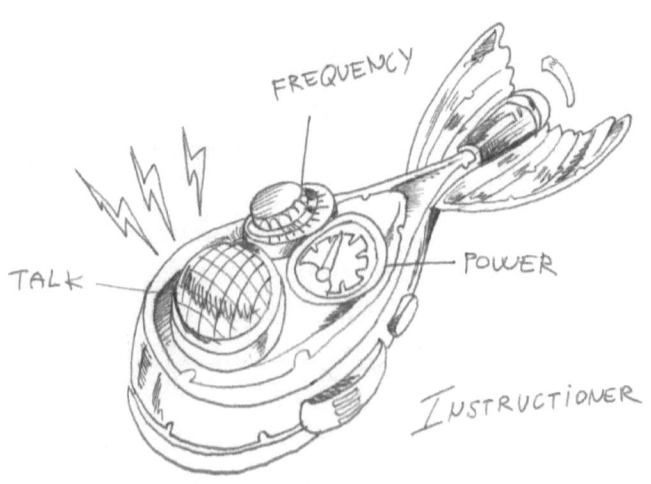

The idea was so uncomfortable to Andy, here he was just making stuff up left and right. He was so far off of scripture not to mention archeology. The things Jonah's instructioner would have needed that weren't available to him were too numerous to count. Advanced materials, electricity, some kind of battery or power source. Solar power was an obvious choice, which Andy began to seriously consider would explain why all of scripture happened in the desert, then he chastised himself, actually shaking his head in disapproval. Of course that had nothing to do with it! None of this was real.

He was so unsettled by the division in his own thoughts that he didn't know exactly what to do next. He looked back at his sketch, proud as he was of it, and as he regarded it more and more intently, he realized that it was growing on him.

An open mind. Maybe that's what an open mind feels like. One to which all things are possible.

For with God nothing shall be impossible. Luke 1:37

The scripture came to mind with force. Nothing shall be impossible. If God wanted to inspire his children to invent plastic, or who knows, some kind of lightweight titanium, he could. And if he wanted to give them a solar cell that was so effective a tiny dot could absorb all the energy you needed – would that be any different than sending an angel to whisper into Jonah's ear?

In both cases, the same principles applied: God had a message for his children, a set of instructions. His servant, the prophet, would receive the message and then have the freedom to follow it. How God delivers the message is quite irrelevant to the ultimate outcome, only that with God nothing is impossible.

Miracle 2 – The Lord causes a mighty tempest.

Andy jumped right into the second one before his brain hurt too much. Maybe this miracle would be easier to invent. And in fact, as he thought about it, it was a pretty easy one to handle. A tempest, as Andy understood it, required a sustained force of wind and some rain to go with it. He wasn't meteorologist enough to know how these two things worked together, but since he was just creating a storm, he needed only imagine some massive fans, say a few the size of a baseball field or perhaps a large number of fans the size of a small house, whatever it takes. These fans just need to be far enough away from the ship that the sailors won't realize that their tempest is exclusive to them. There's no point in creating a storm that covers the whole sea when a local one would do just fine.

That would take care of the wind. The rain is equally simple. Perhaps a tanker perched a short distance away, one big enough to easily manage the storm, one that holds the rainwater in its belly and can pump the water up in front of the fans to be blown into the ship on which Jonah is making his fruitless attempt at escape.

Creating the technology was easy enough – all of these things already existed in Andy's world, though perhaps not in that size, nor would it be easy to position all of these things in the air or on the sea at the right place and time. And then there's the question of how it would all be run.

Angels? They have to do something, after all. Though Andy realized invoking angels was really rather Way Two of him. Feeling empowered by his earlier attempts, Andy tried to imagine an alternative to angels manning the ship.

Robots? Computers? Was there a HAL 9000 on board his tanker ship, perchance? One that wouldn't lock anyone out of the pod bay doors, of course. Since this one would have been programmed by God.

Chuckling audibly, Andy suddenly remembered he was sitting in a glass-enclosed reading room alone and that laughing in such a circumstance was a decidedly nonstandard behavior. Then he chuckled again. Maybe it was a sign of creativity!

The whole exercise was starting to get to his head, making him see fanciful images of large turbines with angel wings holding them aloft above the sea, powered by some kind of solar energy again, or maybe nuclear, who knows? There were too many possibilities swimming around in his mind, each one more interesting than the last.

But none of them true. That much Andy knew. Although that fact didn't make them any less fun to imagine. With this momentum behind him, Andy found it simple to work through the next few miracles.

Miracle 3 – The Lord makes the lot fall upon Jonah.

How could you make this creative? Doodling a bit, Andy tried another sketch, this time of a chooser, a lot-falling device. It was only when he got halfway into sketching a futuristic object that he realized he had drawn a version of the Simon game he had had as a kid. This UFO-shaped game had four colors on it that flashed lights and made sounds which you had to imitate in sequence in order to stay in the game. Once he realized his game was essentially a borrowing from a childhood toy, he was less impressed with himself. But still the idea was an interesting one. Instead of drawing straws or casting dice, maybe the men on board the ship challenged each other to a game of Simon, and whoever lost was the guilty party? A bunch of flashing lights and buzzing sounds would certainly impress the sailors and make them likely to believe a supernatural power was behind the assignation of blame.

This was a cute way to solve the problem, though if he wasn't careful, Andy recognized he was close to breaking the first of the two rules. God still had to be involved in the designation of Jonah as the guilty one. That wasn't hard to imagine, though, because if God could manipulate the straws or the dice as Andy had already decided He could, God could certainly work the mechanisms of the game in order to catch Jonah.

Miracle 4 – Jonah chooses to tell the truth.

After the momentum he'd built up on the prior three, this miracle caught Andy a bit by surprise. It was, in fact, one of the most important of the miracles, it had been the one that had caused his epiphany the day before. But the miracle here required no new technology whatsoever. It just required a change of Jonah's mind. It required that he turn back toward God and do what he had been instructed. There was a deep wisdom to this observation and he had half a hunch that Gordon had planted this idea.

He tried to formulate his observation for maximum clarity. He wrote in his journal:

This miracle depends on nothing other than the freedom of man. No angels, no solar cells, nothing under heaven or from the earth can compel this miracle. For it to be a miracle at all, it must be given freely, from the individual to God. Our responsibility is to repent. His is to forgive.

A residual peace from the feelings he had had the day before washed over him, gently lapping at the parts of his mind that did not fully understand what he was learning. That peace was beautiful, warm, and true.

Miracle 5 – The storm stopped.

Easiest of them all. All Andy had to do was to turn off the fans and stop the tanker from pumping water out. The HAL 9000, or HAL 10000, Andy thought, could do that with a single instruction. And the storm would "cease from her raging." Contemplating this, Andy did wish he had more artistic talent. He could imagine a lovely painting depicting the whole scene, with winged turbines, a tanker ship, all blowing a tempest in the direction of a rickety old ship just a few hundred yards away. It would have to be huge to capture the scope of the operation, exactly the kind of painting old European cathedrals would feature in a side chapel, except that no church would commission an abomination like the one he was imagining.

Miracle 6 – The men make a commitment to follow the Lord.

Here again, another miracle in which the miracle was far more eternal and of more magnificent scope than even the very elaborate storm-making miracle he had just finished envisioning. Though rather than just leave this one there, he did think it was worth contemplating what kind of invention would aid the process of making a commitment. Certainly God had commanded His children to perform their sacrifices over altars, and when you really inspect the Old Testament there are some very detailed descriptions of how the priests should be dressed, how the area should be laid out, and who had permission to be present.

Though it's not something Andy had spent much time on, it did seem upon quick reflection that God prescribed a certain pattern to the promises that were made to Him. From sacrifice to baptism. Though Andy knew of no specific device or object sailors might have used to make their sacrifice while at sea, he could easily see them putting their hands back on the Simon game – it was a silly image, he knew, but a very useful one – to swear their oaths to God. The incongruity of this image with the reassuring feeling it gave him forced him to a new insight which he immediately wrote in his journal.

Who am I to decide how God will ask His followers to make their promises?

He underlined the sentiment as he re-read it. Maybe all of his conjuring of fanciful technologies will have been worth it if it ultimately led him to a mind open to anything God wished to put there. Because if the first instinct after repentance is to covenant to follow God, that is the moment when one should be least insistent on arrogantly telling God exactly how that should be done.

Miracle 7 – God sends some kind of fish to pick up Jonah.

It was time for lunch, but since Andy knew Christine wouldn't be at the pizza place and since he was just one miracle away from completing Way Three, he opted to keep working, offering a silent prayer for Christine that she would do well on her test.

It was a full thirty minutes later that he realized what a mistake he had made. This final miracle, the one that seemed appended to the end of the chapter and was really of little lasting consequence, also happened to require the most creation, the most invention, to make it work.

As he pieced it out, this fish would have to meet several conditions. It would have to:

1 – Be large enough to "swallow" and hold Jonah.

2 – Have life support capabilities for three days and three nights.

3 – Be pilotable by either an automated intelligence or an external party.

4 – Be in the right place at the right time so Jonah wouldn't drown.

There were some implied conditions as well, some that were clearer than others. For example, did the sailors actually see the fish? Did they later corroborate Jonah's tale with their eye-witness accounts? In fact, the text completely omits who deemed the "fish" was a fish at all. This line of thinking led Andy to further ask: Did it even have to resemble a fish or was that just a convenient word that you would use to describe an object that can swim under the surface of the sea and hold a human being?

The most obvious technology Andy proposed was a one-man submarine. This wasn't so much an invention but another borrowing. One of his favorite childhood memories was going to see the movie, *20,000 Leagues Under the Sea* and later having his father read the book to him. True, the huge squid was terrifying to a four-year old mind, but even at that impressionable age Andy had appreciated that the imagination required to envision such an underwater vessel in the late 1800s, as Jules Verne did, was stupendous.

Here he tried to sketch again, but didn't quite have the mechanical aptitude to draw a one-man submarine that would be capable of "swallowing" a man. Reflecting on Way One, however, Andy realized that he had always assumed a certain method of swallowing. First, he counted on Jonah being unconscious or at least waterlogged. Second, he had always assumed that the fish, or whale as he had envisioned it, had taken Jonah by surprise. These conditions could certainly have been true, but there's nothing in the scripture that required them. In other words, when Jonah was tossed into the water, he could have known something was coming to pick him up. How? Using his instructioner, of course! He could have been told what was coming right down to the detail on how to board the vessel.

Thus combining the humility learned from Way One with the creative permission he was granted by Way Three, Andy decided he could envision it capable of either an emergency rescue – the swallowing he had long envisioned – or a deliberate boarding.

This made his submarine have two possible openings, a front-loading bay a bit like a mouth that would open up and capture Jonah and whatever other water or sea creatures were nearby. A simple bilge pump would be necessary to push that water back out through some kind of airlock. It would have to move quickly to keep Jonah from drowning, but that was easy enough to imagine. The other opening would be more traditional, a porthole at the top of the vessel that could breach the surface of the water and allow Jonah to climb up and in. He opted for the front-loading emergency rescue bay for dramatic effect.

Without taxing any nonexistent drawing skills, Andy took time to imagine the basic internal layout of such a vessel. In one scenario, Jonah was a rescued victim who might need resuscitation and even intravenous fluids to sustain his life for three days. No reason to waste electric light on him at this point and since the vessel pilots itself or is piloted externally, it would feel to Jonah for all intents and purposes as if he had been swallowed by a fish. Perhaps he was even only semiconscious throughout the journey, receiving whatever medical attention he needed by robotic delivery of different chemicals, medications, etc. Thus, when Jonah was deposited back on the beach after three days, he very much would have reported to anyone interested that he had been swallowed by a big fish.

The other scenario was equally easy to support with technology available in Andy's time, if not Jonah's. The only difference is that it required Jonah's active participation. Knowing how to board the vessel, how to conduct oneself throughout the process, these should have been foreign steps to Jonah and would have required continual communication – there goes the instructioner again – to ensure he knew how to proceed.

Andy found that although this was the least necessary approach – it would have meant exposing Jonah to a whole range of technologies, materials, user interfaces, things that it was safe to presume were all foreign to him – it was also the more interesting of the two. Because it's easy to simulate being swallowed by an organic vessel, but it's potentially more useful to share knowledge with the prophet in such a way that it confirms how far God's power was beyond man's. Since that was indeed the lesson God intended to teach Jonah at this vulnerable point, it actually made a certain sense to imagine things went exactly this way.

Either way, God made a vessel, or "prepared" it, to use the language of the scripture. And God directed that vessel to retrieve Jonah, sustain him for a period of either learning or darkness or both, and then deposit him where God needed him.

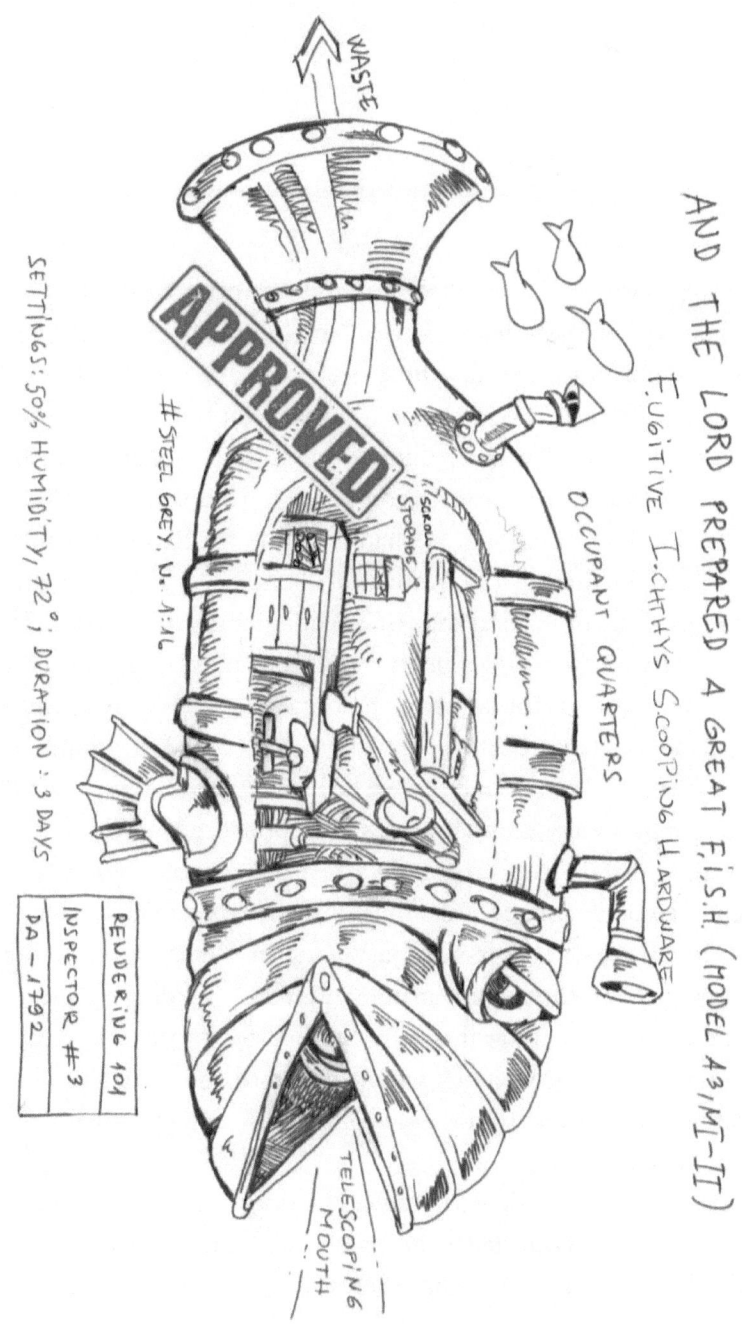

Chapter 8

Andy rang the doorbell. It was the second time in as many days that he had made the walk over to Christine's apartment. Two years into college and for the first time he felt like he was on the verge of having a girlfriend. Though he didn't dare say it out loud, the events of the last few days had given him every reason to think that he and Christine were, if not already, soon going to be a couple.

It was dumbfounding. He had tried the dating thing off and on, but it seemed that all the avenues for finding a girlfriend involved either partying or having lots of spending money or both. He did neither. His method was much more old-fashioned. He would try to be nice to a girl, maybe someone he noticed in a class or at church. If she seemed to reciprocate, eventually he would ask her out. Dinners were expensive, so were movies, so he had a habit of asking girls if they wanted to go to any number of campus-sponsored activities. Come to think of it, he did tend to prefer guest lectures as a cheap form of dating. Maybe that's one reason why his success rate had been so low.

Then there was the issue of just being an average-looking, but nice enough guy. Without the aforementioned spending money. That wasn't the kind of thing that rang the bell for most girls. And Andy would never have expected it would appeal to someone like Christine, a beautiful, intelligent, well-dressed girl who seemed to have everything going for her.

As he waited for her to answer the door, these reflections began to undermine his confidence. He tried to remind himself of the events of the last few days, certainly they were proof that something was working.

The door opened and there she stood. She had obviously put some time into her appearance and now Andy was struggling even harder to find any reason that she would want to spend time with him instead of any other guy. Really, looking like she did now, she could have any guy she wanted.

And I'm supposed to be taking her to dinner? Andy puzzled.

"Hey there," she smiled, with a twinkle in her eye. She didn't invite him in, but instead grabbed her keys and her purse and stepped out the door right into him. He hadn't had the sense to move back, but instinctively reached his hand out to catch her arm so she wouldn't collide with him, but his efforts didn't help. Her momentum propelled her forward right into him, but not before he finally realized that her advance was intentional.

She was moving in for a hello kiss!

His hand slipped past her arm and fell to the small of her back, letting him catch her in a simple and satisfying embrace. She stepped up on her toes and with eyes closed gave him a brief but warm kiss on the lips. There was no missing her intentions on that one. It was a bona fide kiss and suddenly Andy's mind was set to spinning.

Arm still behind her, he supported her as she leaned back, still half on the balls of her feet. She looked up at him from opening eyes, smile as wide as ever.

"Did I catch you by surprise?" she asked, staying comfortably within his embrace.

"Um, no," he began, then, succumbed to honesty. "Actually, yes." The heat in his face rose as he looked at her inviting eyes, smelled the hint of a perfume that he couldn't identify. That he didn't need to identify, really, to know that he was happy to be close enough to smell it.

"I thought it would be easier that way," she explained, resting back on her feet and slipping out from under his arm, catching his hand in hers as she separated from him. "You know, so you wouldn't wonder."

Oh, I'm wondering plenty of things, don't you worry! he nearly said out loud, before he thought better of it.

"Thank you, I guess."

"Don't mention it. I know it can be hard for a guy to know exactly where he stands."

Still don't know! part of him nearly screamed.

"And where is that, exactly?"

"Why, Mr. Harding, don't you know?" she exclaimed coquettishly, pulling him along down the stairs to the main floor of the apartment building. "We're dating!"

And there it was.

"So where are we going on our big date?"

Suddenly Andy wished he had put more thought into this night. He had been uncertain whether it was even a *date* date or just a hangout with a friend. So he hadn't put as much work into his appearance as she had, nor had he resolved where to eat. He had been going back and forth between a diner up the street and a newer Cambodian restaurant that people were talking about. The diner had the advantage of being cheaper as well as less intimidating – he wouldn't be nervous about what to order at a place like that. The Cambodian place would be the exact opposite. More expensive and definitely intimidating. He was from Des Moines, after all. He wasn't even sure where Cambodia was on a map, much less what foods they would offer.

Christine had practically sealed it, though, when she announced that they were dating. Andy had enough sense to know that you can't go to a diner on your first official date.

"I'm thinking The Elephant Room," he said, feeling her grip on his hand tighten as she turned to him.

"Wow, somebody has big ambitions for tonight!" she teased. "I'm all for it, I love a good *amok trey*."

"Yeah, I figured as much," he nodded, smiling back just for the joy of seeing her happy. Hoping she couldn't see right through the fact that he had no idea what *amok trey* was.

~

Andy sipped the last of his coconut lemonade. The food really was amazing. The mix of flavors and textures was just delightful. As long as he pretended he didn't see the prices on the menu he was having the best night of his entire life.

The food was just a fraction of that happiness. Time spent with Christine was enjoyable on every level. They talked about everything under the sun, ranging from their favorite episodes of *Different Strokes* (she did do a mean "What you talkin' 'bout, Willis?" he had to admit) to whether the Berlin Wall would ever come down to why Christine had forsworn wearing two polo shirts at the same time. Despite feeling like he wasn't good enough for her, in her presence she managed to inspire him to believe that he really was someone that she could go out with.

It was a gift she had and he was glad to be its recipient.

But as their meal segued into dessert and they were eating their vanilla ice cream topped with mango slices, Christine reached her free hand out to take his. The gesture was so inviting and natural, yet so undeserved, at least in that part of his brain that couldn't believe his good fortune, that he finally blurted out the thing that had been lurking beneath his thoughts all night.

"I don't know what I did to deserve this," he said, only half realizing that he'd said it out loud. Though the words were a compliment, the way he said it suggested more doubt than appreciation and he worried it would throw a wrench in things.

Looking up at her, he waited for her reaction.

"To deserve what?" she said, in complete innocence.

He set his spoon down and looked at where he had set it. When he was ready he finally looked up at her and let it all come out.

"Don't get me wrong. I'm thrilled. I'm amazed that I'm sitting here, having dinner with one of the most radiant and wonderful girls I've ever met," now he looked away again, "but I don't get it."

"I don't get what you don't get," she said, her hand tensing a bit in his.

"Look," he started, slowly at first, then building momentum as he realized that it was probably best to put it all out in the open. "You are the kind of girl that a guy like me doesn't ever stand a chance with. I hope I don't have to explain that in any more detail. But, it's just that I've spent several years at college unable to really meet anyone half as special as you, and here I am."

As awkward as it was to say, getting it off his chest made him very happy. Either this thing was real and she would put his doubts to rest or his words would cause her to wake up and realize that he was right and it would be over. But if that was going to happen sooner or later anyway, in this moment, perhaps foolishly, Andy wanted it to be sooner, not later.

It was a while before he could look at her again, awaiting her deliberation.

"Andy, I don't know whether to be more flattered or more insulted." Her words were alarming, but they weren't spoken in anger, so he hoped he still had a chance that this would come out well for him.

"I like that you like me, because, well, I like you, so I like hearing that you think I'm someone special." She took her hand away from his and sat back, resting her arms on the chair armrests as she regarded him seriously.

"But I want you to know something about me. I know what I want. And I know what I don't want. Maybe I didn't come to college three years ago knowing all of that, not as clearly as I do now. But what I've learned in years of college is that all that glitters is not gold. I've dated a lot of glitter. There are many future politicians, lawyers, and bankers here. And it seems like they fit into one of two categories: they either just want to have fun, to pass the time while they're in college, or they are looking for their trophy wife that will stand by their side as they accomplish the goals that they've set for themselves."

She paused, ran her fingers through her hair, and looked at him with a grimace, and he couldn't tell whether it was directed at him or at the memory of those boys she was talking about.

She continued, "I can guess what you've been thinking while we've been out to dinner, but based on your question, it's clear you have no idea what I've been thinking. So, maybe I owe it to you to let you know where you stand."

Now she was sounding serious. Andy braced for whatever was going to come next.

"Like I said, I know what I want. And what I want is goodness. Goodness is something you have. It's something I saw in you in class the times you attended our lectures." And for the first time it was Christine who looked flushed. Looking aside, she continued. "I even noticed it in the careful way you handed back papers, I noticed it in the way you did – or did not – look at the girls in the class. And I noticed it in the shy way you pretended not to notice me. Goodness. In all the boys I've dated I have met many boys who will someday go on to do good things. But they'll do good things because they believe they have a right to do good things. Because of who their parents are, or what job they have, or to earn the praise of others. You, Andy, you will do good things because you want to *be* good. And that makes all the difference. To me, anyway."

Her face shone in the light of her conviction. "You, mister, have been on my mind for some time. And when I saw you in the pizza place that day, well, I took it as a sign."

He was speechless. It wasn't his reddish hair, his pale skin, or his gangly tallness that appealed to her, though he knew that already. It was something inside him. Something he wasn't sure he even possessed, but something which he also wanted. And it was a relief to him to know that the thing she wanted also happened to be something he was very committed to having.

"Cat got your tongue?" she said, the sparkle returning to her eye.

He smiled broadly, happier than he had been all night. He really did have a chance with her. He just had to be good.

~

I had a date. With my dreamgirl. It was the only thing he had written in his journal that night before he went to bed. There was too much to process, too much to say, but no actual words that did the experience justice.

Without actually trying, Andy had managed his way into dating the most amazing – and, yes, beautiful, though he tried not to think about that, well, not too much – woman. The choice of word in his mind, *woman*, was loaded with meaning. Until that moment, college girls had been girls. Young, not ready for life, just like himself.

But when he thought of Christine, especially given last night's conversation, he thought of her as a woman. She knew what she wanted, she had said that. And she was ready for life. And for some reason she saw in him her match. Albeit a year behind her in school. Suddenly he seemed impatient to graduate. To become a man in the way he now saw her as a woman.

Rain fell, heavy and scented with the lingering pollens of early summer. The yellow powder ran where the rain took it, coagulating in the gutters, painting the sidewalks with irregular patterns that he stepped around and through on his way to Gordon's office. The professor had indicated he'd be traveling back the evening before so they had never had a chance to check in on Way Three. Arriving promptly at nine o'clock, Andy brought a small bag under his arm, shielding it from the rain, a kind of welcome home present.

Gordon's door was wide open and Andy tapped gently on it before stepping in.

"Andy!" Gordon exclaimed cheerily. "Good, I'm glad you're here. Come in, come in."

"Welcome back, Professor, I trust everything went well?"

Gordon stopped from rifling through piles of paper to regard Andy.

"Yes. Quite well. So well, in fact, that I couldn't sleep all night. I've been in here since before five in the morning."

"I brought you something," Andy offered, extending the bag.

"What's this?" Gordon asked, taking the bag, then smiling immediately before opening it. "You know me well, Andy, you know me well." He reached in to retrieve the two crullers. "Oh, with icing this time? What's the occasion?"

"A welcome home present," Andy said, beaming.

"A very welcome one, indeed," he said, setting them out on their napkins. "I assume the second one is for you?"

"Unless you need it to keep your energy up, you've already put in a day's work, it seems."

"That I have, but I would still prefer to break bread with you than to hog all this pastry goodness for myself." Then, suddenly serious, "Or is the correct term, 'break doughnut'?"

They both laughed and Andy was surprised to see Gordon so chipper. He had left under uncertain circumstances and had returned, well, positively gleeful.

"So tell me, what did you learn from Way Three?"

~

It took time for Andy to get comfortable telling Gordon all of the crazy things he had imagined during his experience with Way Three. But with regular encouragement and many chuckles from Gordon, Andy managed to explain it all, right down to the life support systems he imagined the submarine would have to have.

Though it was freeing to express these thoughts so unabashedly, the more Andy enjoyed it, the less certain he was that Way Three had taught him much. His enthusiasm was noticeably diminished by the end of his recounting.

"What's wrong, Andy?" Gordon asked, intuiting something.

"I don't know, Professor. I just," he paused, uncertain what words to employ, "I don't know if I'm making progress."

The mirthful smile that Gordon has displayed all morning flickered for a moment, transforming into a look of gentle kindness.

"All right, then. Let's go back to the basics. Do you feel closer to God today than you did yesterday?"

It wasn't a question Andy had considered, but the answer was clear upon reflection.

"Yes," though in truth some of that may have been the residual effect of the date last night. Was Christine a confounding variable in the equation? Or was she the answer?

"Good, that's a healthy baseline to compare against. So what do you think is troubling you?"

"I'm not sure I know where this is going. I mean, I felt great with Way One, then my whole world was reoriented with Way Two. But now, with Way Three, I feel like I've just made a bunch of stuff up." This last phrase he unintentionally injected with a note of derision, only realizing it afterward when Gordon stiffened a bit.

"Don't get me wrong, Professor, I'm grateful, I just, I want to know that I'm getting somewhere."

The smile returned to Gordon's face. "That you are, my friend, just not where you think you're getting."

The puzzling reply didn't help.

Gordon continued, "Explain to me where you want to arrive."

It was a thought trap, Andy knew, but one that he wanted to get caught in, thinking it would help. He still tried to outthink it, if for no other reason than to accelerate the process.

"Truth. I want to get to truth."

"*The* truth? *A* truth? What truth do you mean?"

Andy's face darkened. He loved Professor Gordon, he really did, he saw so much wisdom in the man and he felt like the most fortunate person on campus to have entered into his tutelage. But he'd also seen enough reruns of *Kung Fu* that part of him resisted when Gordon started asking questions that led to more questions. Shouldn't there just be an answer at some point?

Finally, knowing there was no way to move forward without taking a step forward, Andy answered. "*The* truth. I want *the* truth."

Gordon regarded him. Could he tell that Andy had chosen to respond at random, not knowing the difference?

"I believe you, Andy. And I think you've made the right choice. If we were working through these Six Ways to Sunday, as we've agreed to call them, as a kind of smorgasbord, a buffet from which you can just choose A Way at the end, then I fear that we would be missing the point."

Andy parsed that out in his head. "Wait, so we don't have to choose one at some point?"

"Oh no, we will definitely have to choose something, yes."

Momentarily flummoxed, Andy thought over the first three ways quickly. They weren't necessarily exclusive, true. You didn't need to just choose one of them. Learning humility, submitting to belief, all of that was useful. And each step had helped him with the later steps, at least so far.

Gordon stepped into Andy's river of thoughts, "And as I've said all along, if we do this right, the thing we'll choose will be *the* truth. Not just *a* truth, but *the* truth."

Andy had started the day on such a high. Now he was just befuddled.

Gordon went on. "Feeling a bit dark now? Feeling swallowed up by the seeming inconclusiveness of it all?"

Andy looked up at him, then replayed what Gordon had just said and got the reference. There was a hint of mischief in Gordon's eye that was both devilish and reassuring.

Andy finally replied, "Are you saying it's time we got out of this fishy situation and swam for the beach?"

~

Way Four: Follow.

Andy looked back at the words he'd written at the top of his notepad. Despite his initial frustration with Gordon's puzzling questions, once the two had gotten to the details of Way Four, Andy's enthusiasm returned. Gordon had pages of notes he'd written in his flowing longhand on the train back from Manhattan. The sheer volume of notes imparted confidence that Gordon really knew where this was going, even if Andy did not. Though he did remember that prior to Monday morning when Andy first shared his whale of a problem with Gordon, there had been no such thing as Six Ways to Sunday. But he proceeded in faith.

Gordon had explained that the next steps for Andy were the same as they had been for Jonah. He needed to leave the fish behind and find the purpose behind the miracles. Sure, Andy had been willing to believe in the miracles – either as written or as creatively reimagined – but Gordon had insisted that Andy now step beyond the miracles themselves.

"I want you to accept this simple premise, Andy," Gordon had sad. "It's that God doesn't waste a miracle."

"I can buy that."

"Good, because if it stands that God doesn't waste a miracle, then it requires that we search for the reason for the miracle."

Gordon had shuffled through his notepad, inspecting his notes, he found what he was searching for. "Andy, I want you to follow the effects of Jonah's miracles."

That's when Andy wrote *Way Four: Follow* at the top of his sheet.

"You've been very patient to spend all this time in a single chapter of Jonah, but we have a few more to get through before this is all over, if we even get through all of them, I haven't figured that out yet. But I'm certain it's time to follow the effects of the miracles contained in chapter one and see what they lead to. Tackle chapter two today with this in mind: What did God accomplish with these miracles?"

Now, sitting on a bench beside the still-damp lawn on what was rapidly turning into a sunny if windy day, Andy looked at his notepad. Besides the heading he had initially written, there was nothing, just blank lines. Gordon had pages of notes, none of which he shared with Andy beyond the simple instruction *follow the effects of Jonah's miracles.*

And so, noteless, Andy pulled out his Bible and read on.

Jonah 2

> *Then Jonah prayed unto the Lord his God out of the fish's belly,*

You bet he did! Andy thought, chuckling aloud before he realized that other people were nearby. How could he explain that he was laughing about Jonah praying in the fish's belly? Already, the first three ways were coming back to him. He noted the word fish rather than whale, and remembered to trust what the words say, not what he thinks they say. He was willing to believe that Jonah really was in the belly of a fish that God prepared for him, but he was also willing to creatively imagine that Jonah was in fish-like vessel. He even saw Jonah talking into the instructioner like some kind of walkie-talkie handset. These things came to him so simply, each one adding to his understanding of this single verse, that he was grateful for what they each brought to him. He didn't feel the need to reconcile these ideas or pick one. He found that comforting.

> *And said, I cried by reason of mine affliction unto the Lord, and*
> *he heard me; out of the belly of hell cried I, and thou heardest my voice.*

Parsing these words, the first thing that struck Andy was that Jonah wasn't blaming anyone for his predicament but himself. He wasn't mad at the sailors who threw him overboard, he wasn't angry with the Lord. Instead, he referred to his situation as *mine affliction*. True, he could mean that in a general sense, like *look what a mess I'm in*, which doesn't necessarily acknowledge his responsibility in the situation. But Andy preferred to read it differently, connecting it to the next phrase, *out of the belly of hell*. That phrase was just poetic genius. Because not only did it locate Jonah in the belly of the beast, but it also put him smack in the consequences of his own action – scripturally speaking, people don't go to hell except through their own choices and disobedience. Unlike in today's world where people use hell, as in *war is hell* to describe any tormented situation, in scripture, hell refers to the displeasure of the Lord against those who disobey him.

Perhaps most important was this phrase, *and thou heardest my voice*. Andy was still trying to adjust to the King James language that he knew Gordon liked so much. The *thee, thou, thine* stuff had not been easy to follow at first. But in this case it was straightforward. *And you heard my voice*. He had long thought that the *thou* language was supposed to be a more formal way to speak to God, as if we were too inferior to Him to speak to Him as "you." Gordon had explained early on that *thou* was actually a more intimate form. That in countries all over the world where they still have formal and informal pronouns – like the *tu* and *vous* in French or the *Du* and *Sie* in German – they always refer to God in the most personal form. In fact, the *Du*, the "you" that Germans use when speaking to family and close friends, is actually the same as the old English *thou*. Which became doubly true, Gordon had explained, when you realized that Germans conjugate *Du* with an -st ending. Andy had never studied German, but he had become fascinated enough by this fact that he learned a few basic German-English cognates that proved the point. "You swim" in English became "Du schwimmst" in German.

This had been more than trivia to Andy's mind and one of the reasons he had taken up reading the King James version of the Bible, other than to just follow his idol's example. Because when he read things like *thou heardest* in the Bible as a child, he hadn't really known if it meant "you heard" or "he heard." As if God was such a special "he" that He had His own special pronoun. Like the ancient Hebrews believed you couldn't say the word Jehovah, or Yahweh, then it stood to reason that you wouldn't want to refer to God too personally. He was that far away from us that common words of address were not appropriate to His station.

Gordon had taught Andy to see a deeper truth there. God was, in fact, closer to us than people might have believed. The special words we used to refer to Him were the closest they could possibly be. Jonah, in crying from the belly of hell, was crying out to someone he knew intimately! He was calling on that same being whom he should have been afraid of and doing so in very personal language.

Despite the fact that God would have every right to punish Jonah for his disobedience. This made the contrast in that phrase all the more powerful. *Out of the belly of hell cried I, and thou heardest my voice.* The juxtaposition of hell, a place that Jonah deserved to inhabit, and the mercy contained in the claim that *thou heardest my voice*, not just the *he heard me* of the first half of the verse, but a personal, direct assertion that a very personal God heard him – that was the greatest witness Jonah could bear of God's direct intercession in his life.

> *For thou hadst cast me into the deep, in the midst of the seas; and the floods compassed me about: all thy billows and thy waves passed over me.*

106

This verse made the point even clearer. Jonah acknowledged that the Lord had subjected him to all of these things – the deep, the floods, the billows and waves.

Then I said, I am cast out of thy sight; yet I will look again toward thy holy temple.

The waters compassed me about, even to the soul: the depth closed me round about, the weeds were wrapped about my head.

I went down to the bottoms of the mountains; the earth with her bars was about me for ever: yet hast thou brought up my life from corruption, O Lord my God.

The poetry was so wonderful that Andy was momentarily taken aback. It started with waves and billows, then led to the bottoms of the mountains and the bars of the earth – whatever that meant, Andy wasn't sure – it was clear that Jonah was speaking in grand metaphor at this point. He was certainly dead, corrupt, as the language put it. Buried beneath mountains and the earth. *Yet hast thou brought up my life from corruption.* There it was again, the use of the personal language of redemption. *You have brought me back from corruption, from beneath the earth.* This had to be a reference to death itself, the ultimate corruption. In these few words Andy began to perceive that the metaphor of Jonah's banishment beneath the water was more than simple comparison to the hell deserved of the sinner.

When my soul fainted within me I remembered the Lord: and my prayer came in unto thee, into thine holy temple.

Andy found himself humming along to the poetry, feeling the surge of faith in Jonah's turn to the Lord, just at the moment he felt his soul giving way. *I remembered the Lord.*

They that observe lying vanities forsake their own mercy.

Andy's humming stopped abruptly. This verse came across like screeching brakes. All of the beautiful meditation that preceded it, only to be caught up short with what seemed like harsh judgment on the liars out there who forsake their own mercy. He didn't want to lose the beauty of the psalm, so he continued on to the next verse.

But I will sacrifice unto thee with the voice of thanksgiving; I will pay that that I have vowed. Salvation is of the Lord.

He had spent more time in the New Testament than the Old but he recognized a reference to the Law of Moses when he saw one. The temple had already been mentioned twice in the prior verses and now the reference to sacrifice. There was something here that Andy could sense was important but that he didn't have the background to comprehend. Jews still observed high holidays like the Passover in recognition of historical moments of deliverance. Jonah was suggesting a similar need to ritually observe his deliverance, though he didn't know exactly how it all tied together. There was something deep there about God's mercy, His temple, and the ritual, but he didn't know what. He would have to note it and talk about it later with Gordon.

¶*And the Lord spake unto the fish, and it vomited out Jonah upon the dry land.*

The paragraph mark at the beginning of the verse signaled a break from the section before it. Even though the Bible was organized into books, chapters and verses, that's not how the original scrolls had been compiled, Andy knew. In our modern world ink and paper were so common that we could waste both of them. But in the millennia before Christ and for centuries afterward, if people had a form of writing at all, the resources to write were scarce. In so many of the earliest scrolls from which the Bible would later be translated and transcribed over the years, there was no spacing, no punctuation, certainly no paragraph breaks. Leaving that much empty space would be a terrible waste of clay, metal, vellum, or papyrus – whatever the material on which the words were captured.

Over the years of transcribing the Bible, scholars had to interpret the original markings that indicated the end of phrases or the suggestion of words that didn't appear in the original text but were implied. By the time the King James scholars were assembling the version of the Bible Andy was reading, they had agreed on specific shorthand markers.

A paragraph mark, the backward, uppercase P paired with a second vertical line, or ¶, was one of them. It meant a place in the text that shows a break in continuity, like a break in time. This was common in the New Testament. In the teachings of Jesus, for example, many of His stories and parables are separated with the paragraph mark rather than beginning a new chapter at each new story.

It seemed important to Andy that the scholars had deemed this single verse worthy of a paragraph marker. It suggested that there was a break in the continuity. The first nine verses of the chapter were part of a single concept. They contained Jonah's psalm, his cry unto the Lord and his song of joy upon his redemption. Yet his redemption hadn't technically happened yet.

It didn't happen until the next verse, a verse separated from the rest of the chapter enough that it required a paragraph break.

What did that mean? Of course, it could be one of those things that had muddied over time in the many translations of the Bible. Maybe something that was written in the future tense in one version got dropped into the past tense by a later scholar who didn't know the source language very well. But Andy resisted that notion. If one of his jobs was to read the text in humility, and another was to believe, rather than rationalize away things that caught him off guard, Andy wanted to seek a deeper truth in the words themselves. Something started to materialize in his mind.

Andy excitedly pulled out his pencil and wrote with emphatic strokes on the paper.

Jonah had faith in his ultimate redemption even before it happened! And that redemption was not just from the belly of the whale, it was from ultimate corruption. God redeems us from the twin foes of sin and death with such infinite grace that we can have faith in that redemption even before it happens.

Andy's mind reeled with how profound this notion was. Part of him wanted to hold back and discuss it with Gordon before getting too carried away, but that warm feeling he had become more familiar with during this week of intense study wouldn't let him. He was forced to appreciate the power and depth of these few words. His pencil returned to his notepad.

Jonah's story is like a key that unlocks a vaster truth than the mere details suggest. But only if we follow the miracle.

Chapter 9

Christine had agreed to meet him for lunch on a break from her chemistry lab. "Same place, same time," she had said and he realized that in under a week they had already established a favorite lunch spot. Though he liked the greasy pizza, he wasn't sure he wanted this to be the place they recalled fondly for years to come. Assuming there would be years to come. Boy, he was getting ahead of himself and he knew it. But it was her fault! There was a metaphor here worth exploring – Jonah had been swallowed by a fish, he was swallowed in thoughts of Christine – the big difference being that he didn't want to be vomited back up on dry land. Thinking this caused the metaphor to crumble. Evidently the word vomit, even if it was just imagined and not spoken, undermined amorous feelings.

He waited for her outside the pizza joint. It was a truly beautiful day now, even if the winds coming over the river from Cambridge were pretty fierce. It was only Thursday and in just four days he had been through a roller coaster of emotions and expectations. His faith was alternately tested and strengthened even as his love life was actually showing vital signs.

His own vital signs picked up as he caught a glimpse down the block of her blonde hair. Would this surprise and delight ever end? He hoped not. She caught his eye and waved, adding a smile that washed him with pleasant thoughts. He definitely hoped this would never end.

When she crossed the street to join him on the corner, her hand was already extended to him and he grew happier still with the thought that she would lean in and kiss him. Taking her right hand in his left, he leaned in but instead of a kiss, got a hug, her left arm wrapped around his waist, her chin buried in his right shoulder. Her right hand enclasped his left hand, interlocking the fingers and gripping tight.

He was taken aback at first, waiting for signs of what to do next or how to feel. He could feel her breathing deep against his chest, as if drinking him in. Her grip on his hand relaxed, the smell of her perfume finally catching up to him.

She inhaled again and let out a satisfied sigh. "I needed that," she said, still nuzzling him, now less insistent than before.

He found himself desperately wishing for two things: first, that anyone he knew would walk by and see this so he would later have proof, and second, that he would know what to do to help her feel whatever she was feeling now for a long, long time to come.

She leaned back at the waist, her lower body still pressed against him as she looked up at him with what seemed like a lazy, satisfied smile. Then, seemingly contented that she got what she needed from that encounter, she stepped back and grinned wide.

"I'm feeling like sausage pizza today!"

~

Once they had their slices, Andy suggested that they walk across Kenmore toward Fenway Park. There wasn't anything going on there today, but it was always a thrill to be near the iconic ballpark. Not that there was a pretty place to sit and eat a slice of pizza, true. But the walk was nice, though windy, and that made for good conversation as they made the most of their lunch date.

Her legs were shorter than his, enough that he walked faster than she did. Something he hadn't really noticed before. She wasn't short, not to his mind, and he wasn't really tall, hovering around six feet even. The difference had only been evident in their few embraces and their even fewer kisses. Though he knew it was a bit silly to think of her this way, he enjoyed the feel of her as smaller than him, of needing his protection. Not that she really needed his protection! Andy knew better than to mention any of this to her, but he also knew enough about human instinct to know that this feeling, this desire to see to her safety, was one of the ways a man felt love for a woman.

As if he needed any more evidence that love was what he was feeling.

Soon they were sitting on a bench along Yawkey Way, the fabled alley in front of the park that became a bustling thoroughfare on game day, with sausage vendors and souvenir salesmen occupying strategic territory on the roadway. But for now it was mostly empty, a place for the two of them to become the center of each other's world.

"How's your chemistry lab going?" he asked, tearing into the tip of his first slice.

"Oh," she replied, mouth already working on a bite of her own, "It's going fine. I don't know why I chose this class to fill out my science requirements. I mean, chemistry is fine and all, but to cram a whole semester into a summer term means you are doing experiments nearly daily."

"It's not really my thing, to be honest," he said, holding his slice up for his next bite. "I got through the required science classes pretty quickly so I could get to my major classes."

"Yeah, I can't really say why I chose this one, but I find that I can like just about any field of study, as long as I understand how it all fits together," she said, and took another big bite.

"How chemistry fits together?"

"No," she continued, mouth still chewing – something about her comfort in talking and chewing made her endearing, either that or he was so smitten by her that she could pick her nose and he'd find it endearing. "No, I mean how it all fits together, like how chemistry fits into biology, how biology is subject to the laws of physics." She swallowed, "And how all of that fits in with sociology and psychology. Gordon's history class, for example, it's just a study of how individuals – each acting out the chemical signals in their brains – work together to construct a society that preserves their wellbeing and happiness." Another bite.

"I mean," she explained, chewing some more, "The writers of the Declaration of Independence said right up front that their hope was to allow people the 'pursuit of happiness.' That right there is the preservation of the individual organism, in the form of security provided by social structures."

This had long been Andy's vision of what a college girl should be like. Beautiful, smart as all get out, and great to talk to. But he had never before imagined that such a girl would be so smart that he would fear falling behind her. He tried to catch up by offering something at her level.

"Is that all it is, then? Just organisms, guided by their chemical and biological makeup? Is that what we are?" It was a bit sophomoric, asking riddling questions like that, but he figured it was better to pose questions than to offer shallow answers.

She tilted her head at him. "Don't say it like it's not a marvelous thing. I mean, it's a miracle that we have the capacity to be this sophisticated, that we're able to self-organize and rise above the animals."

Still admiring her, Andy was suddenly struck with a question that he hadn't pondered yet, much less asked aloud. And that question became urgent the moment it occurred to him, such that he spoke it without really thinking about the ramifications of it.

"A real miracle, as in God did it, or just an interesting cosmic accident?"

His heartbeat intensified as he realized he had assumed since their earliest discussions that they were on a similar page when it came to God. She had known, after all, that he was a believer, she had asked that early on. But he hadn't explicitly asked for her take on the question, only reading into her questions what little he could. And now, sitting on a bench in front of Fenway Park, he was about to get his first notion of an answer.

"If you're asking do I believe in God or not, of course I do," she began cheerily, much to his relief. "But I don't have to only look at it like that."

"Sure," he replied, taking refuge in a big bite of his second slice, suddenly eager to occupy his mouth and stifle the unexpected panic that was stirring in him. He had gone from never having a successful relationship in his two years at college to suddenly dating a dreamgirl. He had never thought through the delicate process of sorting out a girl's beliefs before imagining where a relationship could go. Maybe last year that would have been fine. But during this week of all weeks, the one where Andy was facing his most important crisis of faith, well it was more important than ever to him that he find a girl who would strengthen his faith. And whose faith he could strengthen.

She was very capable of looking at things differently. All of her knowledge of psychology – not just because she was a psychology major, but because she genuinely seemed interested in human thoughts and processes – she could examine something as shallow as an episode of *Star Trek* and identify the philosophical themes behind it. He loved that about her. But what would that mean for her beliefs about God?

He ventured into that territory in the safest way possible. "Were you raised in a religious home?"

"Yes, definitely. I'm a Maryland girl, which is appropriate because I was raised Catholic. You don't get more Catholic than that, I suppose, being from Mary's land."

That was actually a topic that Andy knew something about, given that Gordon's special area of emphasis was early American Christian history, which included some writings about which colonies were founded under which religious beliefs and assumptions. While Americans today liked to think of themselves as living in a country where freedom of religion was practiced, it hadn't started out that way. Massachusetts being one of the most painful examples, with its Puritans who indulged in witch burnings and the persecution of neighboring Quakers. Though, to be fair, some of the Quakers kind of brought it on themselves, since they felt the urge to come preach to the Puritans in the Massachusetts Bay Colony, which frequently caused them to be put behind bars or in the stockades for disturbing the good Puritan communities of Boston.

Catholic was something Andy could deal with. He was protestant himself, comfortable with a variety of protestant creeds, as long as they didn't veer off into the Pentecostal or charismatic realm. He wasn't really comfortable with the fringes of those movements, the speaking in tongues and the faith healing. Fact was, he was pretty open minded about Christianity, which probably helped him in his studies, but also helped him now as he was learning Six Ways he could think about Jonah's story.

"I wouldn't say staunch Catholic," she offered, pulling him out of his thoughts and back to hers. "I think God is in there somewhere, and from my experience He's likely to be hanging out behind the curtain of many faiths. So, yes, I can believe, without seeing how it all fits together."

There was some wisdom in that, he understood. Perhaps it was the same thing that caused him to be a non-denominational protestant. Though he was keenly aware, this week of all weeks, at how risky it was to keep your beliefs so tentative. The difference between not standing for just one thing and standing for nothing was usually no difference at all.

"How about you?"

"I'm Iowa stock, by way of Minnesota. Which, I guess, explains my Lutheran upbringing. You know, as a family, we did the Lutheran thing. It's like a Germanic version of Puritanism, which is how I joke about it with Professor Gordon."

Christine laughed, a hearty laugh that made him smile, though he was not certain if she was laughing with his joke or at it. Her laughter continued until she had to catch her breath.

"I love that image!" she finally explained, catching her breath. "You and Gordon swapping Christian jokes that only the two of you really appreciate." She was making fun of him but she did it so sincerely that it was impossible to take offense. "I will laugh about that image for days." Then she leaned into him, hand on his forearm, "Please promise me you'll tell me about anything funny either of you say next time you meet, or any time!"

"I promise," he replied. The genuine delight in her eyes reassured him some more and suddenly he took pride in the idea of having something to tell her next time they would meet that could extend her delight.

~

"I must admit," Gordon began, leaning back in his chair, eyes squinting in the general direction of the ceiling. "I did not see that coming."

These were not words Andy expected and their sudden arrival concerned him a bit. Gordon just contemplated, eyes squinting ever harder and harder.

"But I like it," he concluded, leveling his gaze back at Andy. "I have to confess I hadn't noticed the bit about the tense change in the chapter. As if the present, the past, and the future were all resolved by the act of God that hadn't even happened yet."

Andy's relief was immediate. He felt not only that relief but a small rush of pride that Gordon would be impressed by his scriptural analysis.

"It seemed worth mentioning," Andy explained. "Or felt."

Gordon cocked his head at him, apparently thinking some more. Either Andy was surprising him a lot today or he was in an extra contemplative mood.

"Felt?"

"Well, yeah, it's like something seemed really important even though I couldn't describe it at first. Then, the more I thought about it, the more it started to make sense, the stronger this sense – this feeling – got. It was like—" he stopped, nervous that he was attempting to make sense of something ineffable.

"It was like something or someone was leading you to this conclusion," Gordon stated, more as a fact than a question. "It just felt right."

"Yes."

"Tell me again the last thing you wrote?"

"'Jonah's story is like a key that unlocks a vaster truth than the mere details suggest. But only if we follow the miracle.'"

Suddenly intent, Gordon leaned forward as if pouncing on an idea. "If you had to say what that vaster truth is right now, without hesitation, what would it be?"

"Jesus Christ," Andy replied, without thinking. Then, considering even a few more seconds, added. "That Jesus's work was infinite."

"Jesus? You got that from Jonah?" Gordon didn't seem skeptical so much as eager to explore.

"I think so. I mean, if Jonah had just been talking about being saved from the belly of the fish, he wouldn't have needed to compare his own situation to the tomb of death and being beneath the mountains." Andy was so energized by his realization that Jesus was at the center of Jonah's psalm that he continued eagerly without waiting for approval from Gordon. "Jonah even thanked the Lord for salvation before it happened precisely because the salvation wasn't from the fish, or even from his specific sin. But from the condition of sin itself!" Now Andy was practically on fire and he looked to Gordon who was beaming back at him.

"That salvation is the very mission of Jesus Christ. That's what Jonah was writing his psalm about!"

"Very good, Andy. I'm pleased you found that clarity of truth in an otherwise subtle story. But you went on to say that Jesus's work was infinite. What did you mean?"

"Think about it this way," Andy replied, suddenly the teacher and not ashamed at his presumption. "Jonah was so confident of God's merciful intervention in his situation specifically but more importantly in his sinful condition generally, that he could speak of his impending rescue – from the fish and from the human condition – in the past tense."

"I like the choice of word, rescue."

"It applies because saving a drowning sailor is a rescue, but it's not really the rescue from the water, as I've been saying. It's the rescue from sin. God rescues us. He *has* rescued us. Even before He sent His rescuer, so firm was His promise of rescue, that Jonah could rejoice in the perfect nature of the rescue, in the perfect nature of the rescuer. In Jesus."

"Tell me why that's infinite."

"Because it applies to anyone, in any time, in any place. Those of us here, thousands of years later, or Jonah, hundreds of years before. Its reach is potentially infinite."

Gordon leaned back in his chair, pulling his notepad onto his lap on which he scribbled some notes very quickly, nodding as he muttered to himself, seemingly forgetting Andy was there. Andy didn't mind, he knew this was a good sign, Gordon was in his professor zone. Eager not to miss out on all the fun, Andy pulled out his own pencil and added to his notes.

The mission of Jesus Christ is infinite. It reaches across time and space, offering itself to anyone who will accept it.

Andy re-read his note and realized what a debt of gratitude he owed to Jonah and a fish.

~

Andy's dinner that night was a frozen burrito microwaved at 7-11. Not the low point of his college career, but pretty close. His dinner out with Christine had cost him plenty and he realized that if he was hoping to keep nights like that coming, he was going to have to trim elsewhere in his budget. True, a can of soup would cost less than the burrito. He would likely be eating a lot of both of those things from now on. And he had no regrets.

The next morning the sky was overcast bordering on gray, actually. But there was nothing but sunshine in Andy's head and heart. On his way to meet at Gordon's office, he considered once again the roller coaster that had been his week. From utter despair to romantic joy. It was disconcerting, but it also made Andy feel so alive. As if this was the week he had prepared himself for for years. Most days, most weeks, most months, really, were so unimportant, so average in comparison. As if you were just marking the passing of time. But this week! This had been a week of big moments, important stuff.

Walking a bit more down Comm Ave, listening as the streetcar jostled down the tracks, he realized that though it felt this way, it was a bit unfair to those other weeks and months. Because the things that were happening this week would not have been possible if he had not spent the prior weeks and months doing what he had done – studying, working, paying attention to the world and really being interested in these things. It was all of that preparation that had put him in this week's circumstances.

For starters, he wouldn't be connected to Gordon if he hadn't been serious about his studies and this particular field of study. He wouldn't have had whatever he had that made Christine interested in him as well. And even the struggle of faith he had been dealing with. If he hadn't prepared himself through years of study and prayer and devotion, he wouldn't have had any foundation on which to place these new things he was learning in scripture.

Andy saw the wisdom in this, even if he really did prefer the excitement of the current week. Somewhere in his brain he hoped he could squirrel away this nut of knowledge, that when things seem to be just humming along, plain as always, it might be because you are preparing for, laying the groundwork for things that were even more important.

I have to remember to write that in my journal tonight, he told himself.

Gordon's door was open and there was some kind of odd music floating out of his office. Gordon sometimes played classical music – which just seemed perfect to stereotype, that the older gentleman professor would listen to Bach or Mozart or something – but this music was nothing Andy had heard before. Andy entered and without asking got his answer.

"Jean-Michel Jarre," offered Gordon spontaneously. "It's French, or rather, he is. Electronic music, I'm a fan." He was standing, fishing through some stacks of paper while glancing up at his bookshelf. The music did seem to have some interesting things going for it, though it was a little weird, Andy thought. The closest thing he could think of was a New Order album or something electronic, though that was more for dancing and this, well, Andy didn't know what it was for.

"Did you ever think," Gordon started, still looking through his papers, talking a bit animatedly for the typically relaxed professor, "that music in heaven will be different? By that, I mean that if it's hard for us to imagine God's thoughts and ways, don't you think that His music will also be different?"

Andy shrugged. "I guess I haven't thought much about music in heaven."

This stopped Gordon. "Haven't thought about it? The idea of choirs of angels has never prompted you to wonder what that sounds like? Andy, you need to start living the Bible, not just reading it. It's one of the things I most look forward to about going to heaven. I have a feeling all of the earthly obedience is worth it just to sit in on one heavenly concert."

Andy smiled. These were moments he would cherish, he knew. These times when it was clear that Gordon was a man of many sentiments, all of them noble.

Gordon reached out to turn down the volume on his tape deck, pulling his chair forward, evidently forgetting whatever he had been searching for in his papers and books. Or choosing to forget it to focus on Andy.

"Are you ready for Way Five?"

Andy sat in the chair opposite Gordon's desk and pulled out his notepad and pencil.

Gordon began. "You've come a long way, Andy. After you left yesterday I considered what we've learned together so far and I was impressed. I'll save my summary thoughts for tomorrow, when you complete Way Six, but for now I want you to make this more personal."

Andy couldn't think of how any of this could possibly be more personal. His whole system of belief had been turned upside down, what else did Gordon have in mind?

"Like I said a minute ago, you need to start living the Bible, not just reading it." Gordon focused intently on Andy, as if sizing him up. Was he weighing his next words, choosing them carefully? It seemed so to Andy. He got his pencil ready.

"Let me ask you this, what's the most oft repeated commandment in the words of Jesus?"

Andy wondered if he should know this. He started recounting basic commandments in his head. Luckily Gordon hadn't said *in the Bible* because that would have been far outside of Andy's reach. The book of Leviticus, for example, probably contained hundreds of commandments and Andy hadn't spent a lot of time digesting them.

Jesus's words, however, Andy was more familiar with. He knew the basics, like *If ye love me, keep my commandments*, which is itself a commandment. *Be ye not troubled*, was one of his favorites, albeit an unusual one. Then there's the—

"'Seek, and ye shall find,'" Andy blurted out, purely because it felt like the right answer, even though he wasn't sure that this qualified as a commandment per se. More of a promise. Which, Andy guessed, was what commandments were anyway, *do X and I'll do Y*.

"Good. That's my read of the commandments as well. Especially when you add in the related, similar sentiments, like 'ask, and ye shall receive.'"

"'Knock and it shall be opened unto you,'" Andy completed the thought.

Gordon nodded and offered a smile. "Why do you think this commandment is repeated so many times?"

"You repeat things that matter," Andy suggested, not sure if he was capturing the whole point.

"True," began Gordon, in a tone that Andy knew meant there was more to it. "Then why does this particular commandment matter so much?"

Andy looked over his notepad, not expecting to find the answer, but to buy himself some time. Gordon had posed a fair question. Why did seeking matter so much?

"It's a bit of a compound commandment, isn't it," Andy started, teasing it out in his mind just seconds ahead of his own words. "There's the commandment, the seek, the ask, the knock. That's our part. But then the second half isn't a commandment at all."

"What is it then?"

"A promise, at least it seems like it. If you seek, God promises that you will find."

Nodding, Gordon prompted him further, "Who does the finding?"

"I guess, saying it that way, I do – or the seeker does, anyway – but it wouldn't be a promise if God didn't have a role in there. As if He was going to ensure that you find what you're looking for."

"I like that, but I want to leave open the possibility that the thing you find may not always be what you're looking for."

Reflecting on this, Andy's hands twirled his pencil a few times. "No, it doesn't promise that, does it, I mean, it doesn't say, 'Seek for a specific thing and ye shall find that exact thing.'"

"Precisely."

"I can certainly attest to that!" Andy exclaimed, suddenly making the connection to his own week of ways. "If I'm honest with myself, on Sunday night, when I was praying about this doubt that I was drowning in, I was seeking the removal of that doubt and discomfort."

"Would have been nice, I imagine?"

With a quick chuckle, Andy said, "At least I thought it would have been nice. But, now that I'm this far in, I wouldn't give up this experience, this opportunity to learn, for anything."

"You are finding, then?"

"Definitely. I'm definitely finding."

"Good, then since you're already confident that you are able to seek I'm going to give you Way Five."

Chapter 10

Andy looked at the top of the fresh, new page in his notepad.

Way Five: Seek

The overcast sky had solidified and the June air had chilled a bit, chasing Andy away from the grass or any other outdoor location. Instead, he wandered through the floors of the library, relishing once more the splendid emptiness it afforded in these summer terms. There were graduate carrels free for the taking on every level as well as large tables that were empty throughout. And there was a marvelous silence which the rows of shelves presided over, as if the books themselves could absorb offending noises and silence any careless perpetrator by their solemn presence.

He had chosen a spot on the north-facing side, overlooking the river. Since the sun wasn't going to shine through the windows on the south anyway, this at least gave him the picturesque Charles River to glance at from time to time. Holed away like this, he had pulled out his notepad and begun to reconstruct where the conversation with Gordon had gone.

Seek the meaning of this scripture to your own life.

This was the easiest summary sentence that Andy could think of, but it was also unsatisfying. There was more to it, even more than Gordon had intended. Because as Gordon had instructed him on how to think about the verb *seek*, it had connected in Andy's mind to the first moments of their conversation that morning.

Don't just read the Bible, live it!

It sounded like a bumper sticker, but it was an effective summation of the many thoughts that had come to Andy while Gordon spoke, so he kept it, considered it, and then added to it.

The story of Jonah and the fish is not really about Jonah at all. It's about each one of us. When we see this, we are not just reading scripture, we are living it, reading to find out where we live in the story — where we are as the story reads now and where we want to be when we've turned to God. We have to seek ourselves in the scriptures, we have to ask what the scripture means to us, we have to knock on the door of revelation, believing that God commanded us to seek, ask, and knock because he intends to answer us.

Andy paused, re-read his words, felt good about what he had captured, and then opened his Bible. By now, the bookmark in Jonah was unnecessary. The spine of his scriptures had grown accustomed to his newfound love of Jonah and the pages practically fell open.

And the word of the Lord came unto Jonah the second time, saying,

Arise, go unto Nineveh, that great city, and preach unto it the preaching that I bid thee.

So Jonah arose, and went unto Nineveh, according to the word of the Lord. Now Nineveh was an exceeding great city of three days' journey.

Chapter three opened neatly with a clear contrast between this time Jonah received a command from the Lord and the last. The word of the Lord came to Jonah – once again Andy had some fun visualizing this, whether it happened by angelic messenger, a voice Jonah heard in his ear or via the instructioner. But this time, Jonah arose and went. Andy paused on the idea that Jonah had to arise before he could depart. The phrase was strikingly similar to another scripture that Andy had always been fond of, one in John when Jesus explains why He does what He does.

But that the world may know that I love the father, arise, let us go hence. John 14:31

In this case, Andy imagined a group of Jesus's disciples sitting at a table or in a living room and needing to stand to *go hence*. In Jonah's case, it was simple to imagine a washed-up Jonah lying spent on the sand, where the word *arise* would have a very literal connotation. And that could be it, certainly. But the similarity between the two instances gnawed at Andy so he took his pencil to paper.

We have to stand up to go forward.

He wrote this, knowing that it meant far more than the words alone conveyed. Fishing for clarity he continued.

Standing up requires setting the past aside, perhaps setting aside other tasks that we thought were more important. Whether we are leaving behind sin or just the distractions of this world, we must rise, not only physically, but spiritually, elevating ourselves to the level necessary to carry out the greater task, the thing God commanded.

Which in both of these cases, Andy realized, was nothing less than the task of salvation.

And Jonah began to enter into the city a day's journey, and he cried, and said, Yet forty days, and Nineveh shall be overthrown.

If Nineveh was such a big city that it took three days to cross it, then Jonah essentially made his way downtown before opening his mouth. This could have been because he was afraid to open his mouth, knowing that the Ninevites had a brutal reputation – they were being called to repentance for a reason, after all. Andy imagined a big city, a circle from the outskirts down to the center of the city. He put a mental pin in that circle representing Jonah's travel from the edge of the city inward, progressing toward the center, over the course of a whole day. He took his pencil and drew a big circle, the same circle that had formed in his mind. Then he added Jonah, situated in the middle of that circle. Fancy took over and with some deft use of the eraser and more strokes of the pencil, he soon had Jonah in the center of a beast of sorts.

The visual was simple and yet suddenly revelatory. Andy filled in more details, capturing Jonah's predicament, having just been swallowed whole and on the edge of being digested slowly.

Jonah went willingly into the belly of Nineveh!

Andy scribbled this furiously, thrilled at the beauty of the comparison. The first time Jonah was swallowed up whole it was because he refused to do what God asked. Probably because being chewed up and digested by Nineveh was a fate Jonah wanted to avoid. But now here was Jonah, deliberately submitting himself to be swallowed by a city that was certain to reject his message and kill him for it.

Except that it didn't!

Andy went to work with his eraser and pencil, crafting a more complete vision of Jonah in the belly of Nineveh. His heart quickened as did his pace, his fingers working to express what he was feeling. He finally stopped to assess his work.

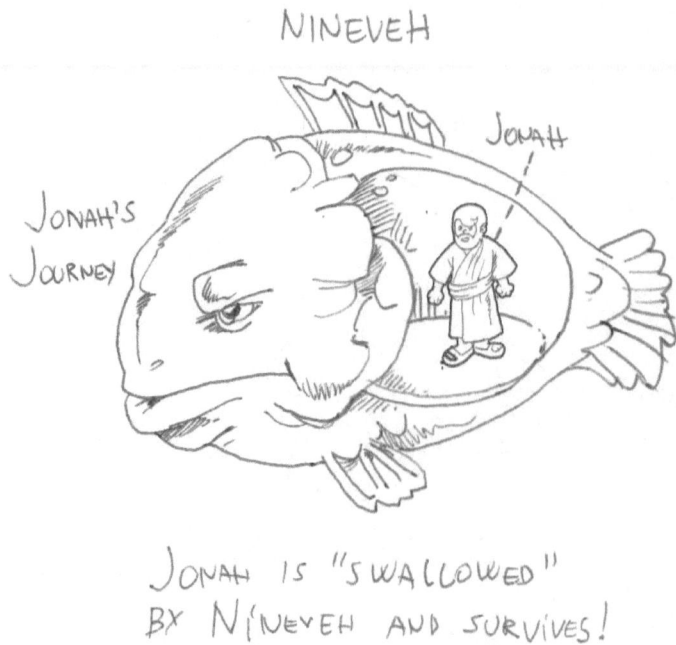

NINEVEH

JONAH'S JOURNEY

JONAH

JONAH IS "SWALLOWED"
BY NINEVEH AND SURVIVES!

The parallels were so clear it was amazing that Andy had never noticed them before. Jonah was swallowed by the fish and presumed himself dead, though he was ultimately set free. Similarly, Jonah was walking into the center of his enemy's capital, certain he would die. Yet he would be set free once again.

A wash of warmth came over Andy as he realized just how much harmony there had been in the seemingly different yet mutually reinforcing Ways he had considered the book of Jonah this week. The Ways carefully and deliberately all added up to the same simple message: God has power over death and hell. And He has given Jesus that power. Over and over the message is taught and retaught, using different symbols that elegantly converge when you set out to consider them in an open way.

He could put the notepad down right there and consider himself finally cured, so strong was the feeling welling up inside him. But he realized that he hadn't yet completed Way Five. He hadn't been seeking to find himself in this scripture. With that in mind, and still riding high from the revelation he felt he was receiving, he continued in chapter three.

¶*So the people of Nineveh believed God, and proclaimed a fast, and put on sackcloth, from the greatest of them even to the least of them.*

For word came unto the king of Nineveh, and he arose from his throne, and he laid his robe from him, and covered him with sackcloth, and sat in ashes.

And he caused it to be proclaimed and published through Nineveh by the decree of the king and his nobles, saying, Let neither man nor beast, herd nor flock, taste any thing: let them not feed, nor drink water:

But let man and beast be covered with sackcloth, and cry mightily unto God: yea, let them turn every one from his evil way, and from the violence that is in their hands.

Who can tell if God will turn and repent, and turn away from his fierce anger, that we perish not?

In a story that is otherwise so sparing in details, these five verses stood out for Andy. They provided a level of information, of completeness, that was missing everywhere else in the story. A simpler way to say it all would have been to end after verse five. Or even the first half of verse five. *The people of Nineveh believed God.* That was the crux of it. That was, Andy recognized, a miracle, on the level of the many miracles he had counted in the first chapter. The Ninevites were the most terrible and fearsome people, so much so that Jonah didn't want to go preach to them. And just when Nineveh had swallowed Jonah completely, when he was a day's journey into the city, instead of, well, digesting him, extinguishing him, Nineveh repented!

While that was all well and good, the verses continued on in great detail about the process of repentance, demonstrating that it was very thorough. In an effort to capture just how thorough the process was, Andy broke apart the verses and summarized the steps.

Verse 5:

Full repentance – everybody was involved.

They fasted.

They put on sackcloth.

Again, everybody was involved, from the highest to the lowest.

Verse 6:

The king personally accepted the call to repentance.

The king arose – arose! – and stepped down from his throne.

He removed his robe.

Then he covered in sackcloth and sat in ashes.

Verse 7:

The king and the nobles proclaimed the fast to all people, including the beasts!

Verse 8:

All are commanded to put on sackcloth

They are to turn, every one, from their evil ways.

Verse 9:

They plead with God to turn away His anger and His punishment.

The list was comprehensive yet compact. Something that Jonah taught these people – we don't know what because we only hear about the promise that if they did not repent, in forty days they would be overthrown. But one had to presume that he taught them about God, about salvation, about the law and the prophets. Otherwise the narrative is incomplete – how can you turn *from* something if you don't know where to turn *to?*

Whatever he taught them, they were ready to hear it and accept it. So much so that everyone received the commandment, starting with the king. This was extremely important in the societies in that region and in that time period. The king was everything. In fact, Andy realized with just a moment's consideration, this fact had largely been the case for every society in any period, at least that he was familiar with. From the chiefs in an old Hawaiian village to the Emperors of the Chinese dynasties, human beings seemed to organize under a leader whose needs and actions became paramount. Laughing a bit at the thought, he recalled that even in a modern representative democracy like England, the Prince of Wales married Lady Di to much national fanfare and celebration.

We don't know this Ninevite king, Andy thought. Was he a tyrant? Certainly he had presided over and probably done terrible, awful things. It was the spirit of the times and the nature of his role. But for some reason, Jonah got to him – oh, how fascinating it would be to sit in that chamber when Jonah preached to him! Was it a forceful, pulpit-pounding, fire and brimstone sermon? Or did angels attend him as he spoke with a still, small voice of the spirit, which caused more change in the king's heart than fiery whirlwinds called down from heaven ever could have?

Whatever happened, it left the king changed. Turned. Ready to act. And act he did.

Arise! That word again, just as Jonah arose from his repentance and days of lamentation, now the king arose, leaving behind the symbols of his worldly power, his throne and his robe. *Arise, let us go hence!* Andy flipped back to his notes from earlier in the chapter to reconsider them.

Standing up requires setting the past aside, perhaps setting aside other tasks that we thought were more important. Whether we are leaving behind sin or just the distractions of this world, we must rise, not only physically, but spiritually, elevating ourselves to the level necessary to carry out the greater task, the thing God commanded.

The symbolism of Jonah's arising and departure to Nineveh couldn't have been expressed more perfectly than in the king's action mere verses later. Jonah had to stand and leave his mistake aside, physically departing from it. The king did the same, leaving his sins and the *distractions of this world*, or in his case, the symbols of his worldly office or power, and elevating himself to the level necessary to carry out the thing God commanded.

Only in this case, the king had to lower himself, not elevate himself. He had to set aside privilege and power and literally sit upon the ground, in a pile of ashes.

This ritual action seemed to be so important, Andy realized, that the king did it as an example, and everybody else did as well, right down to the beasts. Though it was odd to consider asking the beasts to fast,

Andy wondered if that was more a symbolic gesture than a literal one. But the point was clear: Our turn from the sins and distractions of this world must be complete. It must be carried out in dramatic, visual fashion, and it must disrupt our daily lives.

These people had to believe enough to offer a sign to God that His way was above them all.

This emphasis on ritual was certainly something Andy understood. All throughout the Bible the Hebrews practiced numerous rituals – and living in Boston with its thriving Jewish neighborhoods and professional communities had given Andy a fresh appreciation of the power of those ritual observances to this day. Jews still practiced ritual fasting, for example, and he'd had the wonderful opportunity to participate in a feast of the Passover the year before with a Jewish roommate's family.

Modern Christians practiced rituals to varying degrees. The Eucharist was certainly the most common, the ritual observance of the sacrifice of Christ by symbolically taking his blood and body into our own. Catholics, Anglicans, and various Orthodox Christians engaged in still other rituals.

Ritual seemed to be important to people, enough so that they created ritual where rituals weren't expressly commanded. What was it about the power of physically going through an action in order to achieve a spiritual objective? Clearly God approved of rituals, he had commanded them, as Jesus had the Eucharist. And maybe Jonah had expressly commanded the king and his people in how to ritually express their repentance. After all, using sackcloth and ashes to represent repentance or a call for the aid of the Lord was common enough that Jonah may have figured it was the right thing to start with. Or maybe he had been expressly commanded to tell the Ninevites to do this. The mental image of Jonah receiving a message on the instructioner flashed briefly in Andy's mind, causing him to suppress a grin.

Though the Old Testament wasn't really his area, Andy was vaguely aware of what sackcloth and ashes were supposed to symbolize. Thumbing through his Bible Concordance, Andy looked up sackcloth and noted the first reference that came up. It was Genesis 37:34. Not exactly sure what the reference pointed to, Andy looked it up and was surprised at where it led him.

And Jacob rent his clothes, and put sackcloth upon his loins, and mourned for his son for many days.

It was the moment in the story of Joseph when his jealous brothers had sold him into slavery. They had taken his beautiful coat, the coat given to him by his father Jacob, and dipped it in goat's blood. The coat had then been shown to Jacob to persuade him that his favorite son had been killed by some beast.

Jacob's response had been to mourn in sackcloth. This was not a moment of repentance, but a moment of mourning. This cast a new light on Andy's understanding of the idea of sackcloth. He knew that people put it on when they needed to repent and plead for forgiveness, but Jacob had done nothing wrong here. He didn't need to repent.

But he did need to mourn the dead.

A connection stirred in Andy's mind. Death and hell. His realization that Jesus had power over death and hell pressed itself upon Andy's mind as if put there deliberately. Both were corruption, the very corruption that Jonah celebrated being delivered from. One, the corruption of the body – Joseph's death. The other, the corruption of the soul – the sin of the people of Nineveh. The ritual solution was the same, to dress in sackcloth. And the meaning of the ashes suddenly became even clearer to him. The ashes were a symbol of the body reduced to ash after its ultimate corruption in the grave. But a sinner put it upon himself as a symbol of his own sins – his spiritual death.

Another bonus to living in Boston – his first school year in the area had put him in a perfect place to observe Ash Wednesday, the day marking the beginning of Lent. Des Moines not being a particularly Catholic area, he had never seen people walking around his school with ashes in the form of a cross on their foreheads. But in Boston, Ash Wednesday was a wonderful spectacle – faith-inspiring, even for a non-Catholic like himself.

Ashes to remind us, he knew, now that he'd studied a bit since then, of Genesis 3:19:

For dust thou art, and unto dust shalt thou return.

Corruption. The dust represented our ultimate corruption, the corruption of death and the corruption of sin. When the Ninevites sat in sackcloth and ashes, they seemed to be both mourning and repenting. They were morning their own spiritual corruption, as if to say, *We have sinned and we know it.* Which is exactly what they say in verse eight when they exclaim that they need to turn away from the evil they had done.

And by mourning their own sins, anticipating their own spiritual death, they could begin to repent. Just as Jonah did when he mourned his own descent below the waters and into the darkness and under the *bars* of the earth. Only with one crucial difference.

Jonah had simultaneously celebrated his deliverance even as he mourned his corruption.

Andy realized that there was no such confidence in the words of the Ninevites. They seemed to accept that God had the *power* to deliver them, but they were uncertain that he had the *will* to do so. They did not yet believe.

Flipping back to the book of Jonah, Andy read the tenth and final verse of the chapter.

¶And God saw their works, that they turned from their evil way; and God repented of the evil, that he had said that he would do unto them; and he did it not.

The verse stood out to him with such clarity, as if his eyes had been transformed and he could see with eyes of the spirit. The meaning of what his eyes saw rushed into his mind rapidly, so that a sequence of significant thoughts occurred to him simultaneously. Had he tried to write it as it came to him, it would have come out as a jumble, more like a ball of words than a stream of them, the sense of them clear in his soul even if they were not yet clear enough to articulate.

He half expected that under the power he felt he could look around and see angels intermingling with the people in the library. As if he could look up into heaven and see the kinds of things Stephen saw in vision at his stoning.

The moment, as blissful as it was, began to subside. Andy was electrified by the feeling it left in him and wanted to just savor it, yet he was eager to parse the ideas into concrete conclusions he could write down and work to understand.

There's the paragraph mark again! It's a break in the action, a space in the story where something happened. What transpired there? Did the people spend their forty days in meditation and prayer and learned how to believe? Did the days they spent turning away from their old behaviors and toward new behaviors provide ample demonstration to God that they understood their relationship to Him and what it meant for their futures? Either way, whatever happened there, we end this chapter with a single verse denoting a separation between the actions of the people and the consequences of their actions.

The idea that God *repented* of the evil he was going to do often confused first-time readers of the Old Testament, Andy knew. But he'd studied it enough to know that in the Hebrew of the Old Testament, repentance referred to *turning away from* something, just as the people earlier in the verse had to turn from their *evil way*, now God could choose to repent or turn from the *evil* he promised them.

Evil was also a slightly tricky word in the Old Testament, Andy was aware. Today, in English, the word evil referred to an internal characteristic of a person or an act. If someone is evil, it is because they are bad on the inside. The James Bond villains are evil – they want to control or destroy the world and so on. Or we might determine that a child abuser is evil. Even the similarity between the word evil and the word devil was used by Christians in a way that confounded the two. But the words weren't actually related. They originated in different roots, which Andy hadn't understood until he learned in his college Spanish class that devil comes from the Latin, as in *diavolo* or *diabolo* in modern-day Spanish, while evil comes from Old English and German, which was *uebel* or *ueffel* and then eventually *evil*. Appropriately, the word *evil* was used interchangeably with the word *bad* for hundreds of years. A person could be bad, true, but they could also just do bad things without being a bad person. External events could be bad or evil, too, without them having a purpose. If a tree falls on your car, it's a bad thing, and a few hundred years ago, it would have been an evil thing, in the old sense of the word, but not an evil thing in the modern sense. Over time the words bad and evil separated in English and evil took on its modern use.

Add all this up and instead of reading that God had to repent of evil, thinking of all those words in their modern sense, it should instead read that God turned away from the bad or harmful things He threatened to do to the Ninevites. When God warns us that our ways will lead to destruction – a bad thing, when considered from the perspective of the people being destroyed – then when God has mercy on us and turns away from that bad outcome, it is evidence of His true character and attributes.

That's why this particular phrase in this verse was a bit unfortunate, because the way language had changed over hundreds of years, the very straightforward resolution to the chapter – God saw the repentance of the people, He had mercy on them and withheld His wrath – was lost in the translation.

And it was that clarity, that finality, *and He did it not*, that had held Andy spellbound in this moment of bliss as he pondered the three key elements of this single but critical verse.

A space of time passed.

God observed the repentance of the people.

God forgave them.

A sentiment tugged at him. As he wrote out those words, trying to capture their sequence and importance as clearly as possible, he had nearly written *God observed the repentance of* His *people*. He reviewed the verse, thinking maybe he had seen some reference that would suggest God had taken claim of the people. It did not. Yet the sum of what he felt indicated that God was making them His people. Through their belief, through their repentance or turning away from their evil – the harm that they were causing to others but also to themselves – God forgave them. And in the process, they became His people. It felt too true to pass up, though Andy realized he couldn't prove it to anyone else if asked. Still, he added to his list.

God made them His people.

Now it felt complete.

And now Andy felt complete. Because he understood. He had spent this chapter seeking and now he was finding what he didn't know he was looking for.

He was the people of Nineveh.

Gordon had told him to seek what this story means for him, to make it applicable to his life. This was how he fit into the story. He wasn't Jonah. Instead, he was the people of Nineveh. He was capable of evil – maybe using the old sense of the word more so than the present sense – and he had to turn away from that evil. But not just turn away from it, he had to turn toward God. In any Way he could.

Turn to God, any Way you can! Andy wrote at the bottom of his notes.

Then God, observing Andy's turning, would forgive him, redeem him from the twin corruptions of death and hell, and make him one of God's people. God would choose Andy.

A tear welled up in Andy's eye and despite the blurred vision, he could see more clearly in that moment than he had ever seen before.

Chapter 11

The walk to Gordon's office passed in a blur, Andy's feet falling lightly on the pavement. Before he knew it, he was approaching the professor's office for their appointment. He tapped lightly on the door and, forgetting himself, started to open it without waiting for a response. The door was locked, however, and the unexpected resistance of the doorknob left Andy momentarily stunned.

Reflexively checking his watch to make sure that he didn't have the time wrong, Andy started to calculate things he might do nearby while he waited for Gordon to arrive. He reflected on today's lesson, summarizing in his mind what he had learned, how he had found himself in the book of Jonah, without knowing what he was looking for. He was excited to share with his mentor that he had indeed found what Way Five had promised.

Footsteps could be heard down the hall, just around the corner, but there were more than two feet echoing so Andy didn't expect Gordon's feet to be among them. He was genuinely surprised when, in fact, Gordon emerged from the hallway and turned to face him.

"Andy, hello!" he exclaimed, rather enthusiastically, which was not uncommon for him, but still seemed a bit louder and more energetic than Andy expected on a Friday afternoon.

Trailing behind the professor was a young woman with raven-black hair. Though nearly a head shorter than Gordon himself – the professor was rather tall – she still stood out as notably tall for a young woman. Her striking hair was hanging half in her face and her eyes were downcast.

"I'm sorry I'm late. I would like you to meet someone," Gordon said, joyful tone unabated, as he pulled out his keys and began to unlock the door, partially blocking Andy's view of the young woman. "This is my granddaughter, J.L."

She lifted her eyes in his direction and with a practiced motion of her head both flicked the hair out of her eyes and managed to nod at him, mouthing a slight, "Hey," before bringing her chin back down and twisting her closed mouth into a tight knot.

"Hi," Andy said, lifting a hand in a pathetic wave. "I'm Andy."

"Yeah," she said, stopping there.

Gordon had opened the door and stepped back, motioning for his granddaughter to enter his office. She stretched past him and stepped through, showing Andy her long, baggy combat jacket and her torn, bleached Levis. Her feet sported Converse high tops, one green and one purple, with bright red laces. Though typically oblivious to these things, Andy noted these details purely because of the contrast they suggested between her new wave style and her grandfather's conservative manner.

It's not that Andy was surprised that Gordon had a family. Of course he knew that Gordon had had a family – he had lost his wife to cancer just a few years before Andy's Freshman year at BU. And Gordon had pictures of his daughter's family in his office, pictures which Andy had looked at more than a few times. But those pictures seemed far away from Andy's experience of Gordon. The professor never brought his family up and Andy, he now realized, had never bothered to ask.

Yet, here was living evidence of Gordon's family and Andy didn't know where to put that information. It was made even more complicated by the fact that this tall young woman standing in Gordon's office was nothing like the little black-haired girl that Andy could now see in the picture on Gordon's bookshelf. It was obviously an outdated picture. This girl and that girl seemed to be years away from each other in more than one sense.

J.L. looked distractedly at the bookshelves and the various plaques on the wall. Andy tried not to look at her too closely – was that a blue sheen to her black hair? Instead, he focused on Gordon, awaiting any instructions on what would happen next, given the arrival of this new guest. Part of him wanted to generously offer to leave the two of them alone, and that was probably the right thing to do. Yet another part of him also didn't want to miss out on the chance to share with Gordon all that he had found.

Gordon, settling in, looked up at his granddaughter. "J.L., sweetheart, what do you want to do? Andy and I will just be a moment, and you're welcome to stay here in my office."

Looking back around at her grandfather, possibly with a raised eyebrow, though it was hard to say for sure with the hair in the way, she replied, "I'm fine with whatever."

There was a pause and nobody said anything.

Andy took this as his cue. "You know, Professor Gordon, I'm happy to meet later, I mean, if you and your granddaughter want to catch up?"

Gordon, still looking at J.L. who had turned away to regard the bookshelf with feigned interest – or actual interest, again Andy couldn't tell – lost a bit of the chipper manner he had before, but still didn't speak. Then, he seemed to remember something, looked at his own watch and quickly sprang to life.

"Actually," he began, hands pulling through some papers, "I forgot I have to get some forms to the department office before it closes today at four-thirty, I'm going to have to—"

"Let me do it," Andy spontaneously volunteered, resolving that the bigger thing to do was to leave the professor and his granddaughter to themselves. The department office was in another building and the hike over there was one Andy knew well from his days as a TA.

"That's kind of you," Gordon replied immediately, putting his hands on the manila folder with a few sheets of paper, "but unfortunately these are student confidential, I should really deliver them myself."

J.L. turned back away from the bookshelf, shoving her hands in her jacket pockets, ready to follow.

"J.L.," Gordon began, then stopped himself turning to Andy with a sudden thought, "Andy, would you mind keeping J.L. company for a few minutes while I run these to the department office?"

It wasn't quite what Andy had in mind, but he responded with a quick yes, not looking too long at J.L. to see if she was okay with that. From his side glance, however, he realized that there was indeed a sheen of blue to her black hair.

"J.L., baby, you okay if I leave you in Andy's good care? It will just be a minute."

"Sure," she muttered, hands deep in her pockets.

"Great, thank you," Gordon said quickly, realizing he needed to get moving pretty soon. With that, he was out the door.

Andy shuffled a bit, setting his bag down and turning to J.L., who had started looking at the certificates on the wall. Without realizing it, Andy soon had his hands in his pockets as well, trying hard not to look too foolish.

"So, you from somewhere close by?" Andy asked, at a loss for words.

"Indiana," J.L. replied, not elaborating further.

"That's cool," Andy said, aware that he was now officially making terrible small talk.

"Jayelle is a cool name," he added, confirming his sad suspicion about himself. She didn't reply. "Is that, like, *Jayelle*, with an *e-l-l-e* on it?"

This caught her attention, though clearly not in a way that pleased her.

"No," she snapped. "It's two letters, *J* and *L*."

At least when she said this, she turned to face him, flicked her hair out of her face and demonstrated some personality. Mission inadvertently accomplished, Andy figured. Looking at her more closely, he saw eyes that were piercing, and somewhat distressed. Eyes that recently had been crying, Andy realized, and felt embarrassed that he had already judged the girl's attitude from just the few things he had seen. He didn't know her, he didn't know what had landed her on this particular shore. He didn't need to judge her blue hair and her torn jeans.

"Sorry," he said, not sure exactly what he was apologizing for but realizing it needed to be done.

"It's fine, I get a lot of flak for my name."

"What does it stand for?"

"Jay Lee." She didn't elaborate, but Andy's wheels started to turn. Jay was Gordon's first name. He assumed there was a connection. But the Lee, he had less to work with there. Finally, she rescued him.

"I'm named after Granddad and Grandma Gordon both. He's Jay and she was Lee." A brightness came into her eyes. It seemed she liked them and liked being named after them. Which was good because he wouldn't know how to feel about her if she didn't respect the man he had chosen as his mentor.

"How about you?" It was her first question for him.

"Me?"

"Yeah, Andy, right? Where does that come from?"

"Oh, yeah, the Bible. I'm Andrew originally."

"Your parents are religious, too?" Here her tone went down a notch.

"I guess so. Though they're not like pastors or anything, though my mom does teach Sunday School."

"That's religious enough."

"Sure, yeah," was all he could manage. Desperate to change the topic, he went back to something where he felt more confident. "Well, it's a good name. I mean, Jay, at least. Not that Lee isn't." What a fool he was managing to sound like, he realized. "I just mean that your grandfather is one of the best men I've ever known."

"Yeah, totally," she responded, with another flip of her hair, casting her piercing eyes back to the bookshelves.

He followed her gaze, mostly because he had no idea what to say next. He started to calculate a way to excuse himself from the situation, but he didn't want to be disrespectful to Gordon who had left them together. Realizing he was holding his breath in indecision, he exhaled in a bigger sigh than he expected.

This caught her attention and she looked up. Even with her hair hanging in the way, he could see a smirk on her face. "That bad, huh?" she asked, her face cracking into a full grin at that point.

He chuckled in response, still uncertain about how to proceed, but somehow a bit more relaxed now than he had been just minutes before.

"Yeah, I guess so," he replied. He set his pack on the ground next to the desk and felt himself loosen up even more. Rolling with that mood, his courage to speak increased.

"So you come here often?" he asked.

She went from a grin to a chuckle, her shoulders actually shaking. Now he was nervous again, not understanding what had set her off. He tried to reconstruct what had just happened when he realized—

"No, I didn't mean, oh, jeez, I can't believe I said that."

"Worst pickup line ever," she said, still laughing. "I thought you Boston types were supposed to be more sophisticated." Now she was genuinely chortling and all at his expense.

"Okay, forget I said that, I just meant, I just," he stammered his way around his original words. "I just meant if you—"

"Relax, college boy," she said, still grinning, but no longer laughing at him, her eyes firmly pointed in his direction. "I know what you meant," she explained, tipping her head forward and looking at him a tad condescendingly. "It was just funny, you have to admit you did that all to yourself."

Now he finally laughed, the flush of his cheeks starting to cool a bit. "That I did," he said, shaking his head. "Maybe the actual Boston types really are smoother than that, but I'm a Des Moines guy," he said, excusing himself. "We don't pretend to be more sophisticated than that."

"Wow, Des Moines?" she asked, her grin sharpening. Though he knew it was laughing at him, not with him, the grin was at least a pleasant change from the moody cloud that had accompanied her there.

"Go ahead, fire away," he offered, inclining his head slightly and opening his palms as if resignedly bracing for impact.

"No, no fire from this end," she quickly countered. "I mean, anybody who would *admit* that they're from Des Moines earns points in my book," at this she broke into another chuckle. Her warm voice was melodious and he was pleased to realize that his initial nervousness had completely evaporated.

~

By the time Gordon returned, the two of them were idly chatting about whatever came to mind. Knowing that she was family to a man Andy admired somehow made it easier to treat her as a person and less as a girl he should feel his normal level of uncomfortable around. At least after the first few awkward moments. He liked seeing her talk in what seemed like a happy manner because it contrasted with how she had seemed when they first walked in the room. He wasn't sure he could have managed anything more than a few words with her in that state.

When Gordon walked in Andy had practically forgotten about the purpose of his meeting. His chat with J.L. – he mentally spelled her name so as not to forget it – had washed away the urgency of what he wanted to share with the professor. Plus, lingering in the back of his mind were pleasant thoughts about being with Christine later tonight. That was enough to put a smile on his face and a warm buzz in his chest.

"I see you two managed just fine," Gordon began.

"Yeah," Andy replied, "we're good, we've compared names and home towns, so we've covered the bases." His flippantly buoyant tone surprised even himself.

"Good, I didn't mean to leave you in a lurch, but getting those papers in was necessary, so thank you for your patience."

Gordon moved into the room and to his desk, where he began retrieving a pad. Looking up at his granddaughter, he seemed to consider his options, then finally spoke. "Sweetheart, what do you want to do? Andy and I have a few minutes of notes to compare, then you and I can go home and get you set up, get some dinner, all of that."

Andy was amused that the man who spoke with such authority and an air of spiritual knowledge now just sounded like a regular person making plans for the night. It wasn't a Gordon he interacted with much and rather than lessening his authority in Andy's eyes it actually increased the man's credibility.

While Andy considered this, J.L. was busy rifling through her backpack on the floor. She retrieved something from it as she answered. "I'm totally cool back here, I'll just put on Crowded House and tune you guys out." At that she untangled her headphone cord and pushed play on her knockoff Walkman.

While she listened, the sound leaking out of her foam headphones just enough that it sounded like a flea circus playing some distant music, Andy gave Gordon as succinct a summary as possible. He explained how he had sought himself in the scriptures and how he had found what, to his mind, was his actual place. He wasn't Jonah, the individual who needed to hear God's command and go preach to the people. He was the people of Nineveh. Even as he explained it he re-experienced a slight memory of the unique, almost revelatory feeling that had come over him when he first realized who he was in the story.

Feeling that great wave of knowledge wash over him, he concluded his summary. "Now, Professor Gordon, I feel like I need to arise and turn away from my ways and turn toward God's."

He paused, letting the last of the feeling retreat back out from him like a gentle tide. There was a space of silence that Gordon did not rush to fill, scribbling notes on his pad, the silence mildly punctuated by the flea circus of J.L.'s Walkman.

Gordon finally rested his pencil and looked back up at Andy. "There is great wisdom there," he said. His face seemed calm like a summer morning as he spoke, the authority Andy was used to coming back to his voice. "Great wisdom, indeed."

Jay Lee

"Andy, you've been through so much this week. I want to commend you for considering all of these Ways. And you're almost there. One more day, one more Way." He leaned back in his chair and considered.

"With J.L. here I am not certain how my schedule will work out tomorrow. Her arrival is," he paused, "a bit unexpected, though very welcome. Because of that, I would like to spend some time writing up Way Six for you. You could come by the office and pick it up tomorrow morning even if I'm not here. But I am unlikely to be able to be here for an afternoon debrief. I'll leave you some notes for you to consider that as well. Then we can talk on Sunday afternoon if you're okay with that?"

Andy's mind was racing over the implications. He contrasted his feelings in the present with his feelings from just five days before. Where he had been desperate he now felt a sense of confidence. He had a feeling that come Sunday morning the day would break with him ready to embrace Sunday. He couldn't imagine it any other way and he had Gordon to thank.

"That works great, Professor. Thank you."

He began to grab his things and put his stuff away. Gordon, meanwhile, caught J.L.'s attention and motioned to her. She clicked the stop button and pulled her headphones off.

"J.L., I think we're ready to go, we can finally head to the house. What are you in the mood for dinner-wise? We can stop at Chinese on the way if you'd like."

"Chinese sounds cool," she replied, standing up and putting her stuff back in her backpack.

Gordon paused, his face brightening quickly, then turned to Andy. "Andy, you interested in Chinese food? We'd be happy to have you along."

Andy paused, uncertain. Gordon had never invited him to dinner before in all the time he'd known the man. Of course, he'd also never had a young granddaughter to entertain. Andy was torn between his desire to interact with Gordon as much as possible and the awkwardness of having to spend more moments stuck between the two of them. When suddenly he realized he had a better offer.

"That's very kind of you, but I have plans tonight," he said, more quickly than he intended and with a broader smile on his face than even he realized.

"Oh?" Gordon asked, smiling back, evidently sensing something. "Something going on at the dorms?"

"No, er," stammered Andy. "I have a date."

The words hung there and from the corner of his eye he was certain he could see a smirk on J.L.'s face.

"That's too bad," Gordon said, immediately recalling his words. "Of course, it's not too bad that you have a date, it's wonderful that you have a date." He said the words too reassuringly but the fact that Andy had never really had a date in his years of college was a fact that was probably not lost on Gordon. The reassuring tone, meant to be encouraging, just seemed patronizing.

"With Christine Campbell," he blurted out, trying to prove he really was going on a date.

This stopped Gordon in his tracks, and was that surprise on the man's face?

"That's wonderful," Gordon intoned with a firm grin and the full authority of his voice. "I hope you have a delightful evening."

Me, too, thought Andy, offering a polite wave to J.L., saying goodbye to Gordon, and turning on his heels to go.

~

For their second real date Andy hoped it was safe to go to the diner. He'd have to eat soup from a can for several weeks after their last meal at the fancy Cambodian place. Plus, the diner had a certain charm, a kind of 50s quality to it that he hoped would seem eclectic to a well-heeled girl like Christine.

As they walked down Beacon Street, coats buttoned up against the crisp breeze of the evening, Andy's mind raced forward and backward. He was holding hands with this stunning girl and remembering every happy minute of their week together while at the same time flashing forward to what life could be like, a month from now, a year from now, and even beyond. He kept trying to rein his thoughts in, but it was nearly impossible. The future unfolded before him with thoughts that were so joyful it was hard to ignore the possibility that in Christine he may have found the one woman he would want to spend his entire life with.

The only other thing that brought him that much joy was the knowledge he was gaining in this week of spiritual growth. Each day, each Way, had elevated him to a new place. His work earlier today in the library on Way Five had solidified his understanding of who God is, what Jesus had done for him – for everyone – and that knowledge had filled him like a cup brimming to overflowing. That these two immense joys – his budding love for Christine and his deepening faith in Christ – had both come to him in their fullest measure in the same week had to be more than coincidence, wasn't it?

They made it to the diner, pausing in their conversation to pick a seat in the modest establishment. She was answering his questions about her chemistry exam from that afternoon and he smiled as she described how she thought she did. Of course she did well, he had a feeling that she always did well, but she was either humble enough or just very practiced in the art of obscuring her own accomplishments, that she described the test as challenging.

As she talked and he smiled at her pleasantly, she suddenly interrupted herself.

"What is it?"

She paused, expecting an answer to a question that he wasn't sure he understood. After fumbling for a minute to see if he had missed something, he finally gave up.

"What's what?" he asked her back, his face still grinning but his look slowly shifting in a perplexed direction.

"You're somewhere else!" she accused him, gleefully but insistently. "I can see it in your face when I talk."

"No! I'm listening, I promise," he shot back, nervous that she saw something he didn't.

"I know you're listening. I can just tell that you're simultaneously processing something else." As she said this she reached across the faux marbling of the formica-clad table between them and placed her hand on his. "I just want to know what it is."

Gulp. He didn't know whether to tell her the truth – how do you tell someone on their second date that you can almost see eternity in their eyes? While it sounded romantic on the one hand, Andy knew that it also sounded crazy with a capital C. It wasn't the only thing on his mind, true. If he wanted to tell her a truth, just not this one truth, he could share with her what he had found out through Way Five.

"I dunno. I guess I have some things in the back of my mind, things that I learned today in my work with Gordon."

"That sounds interesting, spill it. I'm bored of chemistry for now anyway." She smiled, tightening her grip on his hand and he leaned forward to make it easier for her to continue holding his hand.

"I'm just coming to understand some things that I didn't know I didn't know, you know?" He chuckled, realizing how circular what he just said was.

She laughed a warm and inviting laugh, making him even more comfortable. "I do know!" she nodded, encouraging him to continue.

"It's, well, it's just interesting that I thought I was a believer before. But after just a few days wrestling with Jonah I've found so much more there than I ever would have expected."

Christine cocked her head and tightened her eyes a bit. "Really? This is the same Jonah I'm thinking of, the odd story stuck in the middle of scripture with very little context?"

It was a question that stunned him slightly, mostly for its slightly adversarial tone, though he didn't perceive that she was trying to pick a fight with him. Instead of seeing it that way, he chose to take her at face value.

"True, it is kind of an odd story. But it's also strangely powerful. I mean, packed into these few chapters are a lot of what seem like perfectly planted hints about bigger concepts, about more eternal things."

"Tell me what kind of things," she invited, her smile warming back up.

"Like, did you ever notice the parallels between Jonah's journey to the center of the fish and his trip to the center of Nineveh?" She nodded at this, seeming to appreciate the literary device. "In one case, he gets swallowed and rejected, in the other, he gets swallowed and ultimately embraced. The rejection came when he rebelled, the embrace came when he obeyed." He found that the words to describe this particular lesson came so fluidly, as if it was a truth just waiting to be explained, and some of the joy that he had felt while studying earlier that day came back to him.

"I like that. There's definitely something going on there. Clever."

Though she was approving of scripture, the fact that she was engaged came across as a personal compliment to Andy.

"You know, and today I completely changed what I was getting out of Jonah. I mean, all along I thought that I was reading Jonah as an example or a pattern for a righteous life. If you are a believer, you become a Jonah who is willing to do what God asks, that kind of thing." Her hand felt so warm on his that he was momentarily distracted. "But after reading the account of the people of Nineveh, I feel very differently about it. I'm not Jonah at all."

"You're the Ninevites," she finished for him.

"Exactly!"

"Interesting, I hadn't thought of it that way, either. Though I get it. It's hard to be Jonah because we're not really prophets – or at least I'm not," she giggled as she said this last part. "But anyone can be a Ninevite. All we have to do is respond to the word of God in faith and humility."

She was so on, so right there, that Andy was astonished she could get all that without having spent the afternoon in the library thinking it through. This awareness of her apparently innate spiritual intelligence brought a smile to his face, but his deepening grin was more a function of how smoothly his two great joys were integrating.

His feelings for Christine, his love of God, all coming together into a single great experience.

Riding this wave of feeling he then added the most significant lesson from today's study.

"And I learned that what Jesus did was infinite in its reach."

She screwed up her mouth a bit, cocking one eye. "What do you mean?"

"It's just amazing how thoroughly the mission of Jesus was foreshadowed in the story of Jonah. From the symbol of Jonah's burial in the grave and his rising again from that symbolic death – even born again, like at baptism, wait that's something I didn't even realize was in there yet. Wow!" This thought took him aback for a moment as he realized that this was the burial in water that Paul had spoken of in his epistles. He was getting goose bumps.

"That's really great," she said, her face having smoothed over as she watched him calculate the implications of this thought. "But, hey, it's time to order some food, huh? What do you recommend here?"

Still thinking through the seemingly innumerable references to Jesus in this small book tucked in the middle of the Old Testament Andy finally awoke to the fact that his date was changing the subject.

"Oh, sure, yeah, well, I'm a Reuben guy myself."

~

The evening went remarkably well. Andy found himself so comfortable with Christine, his words came so fluidly, their playful affection sweetening their every topic of conversation, punctuating their connection with reassuring touches. By the time he paid and led her out the door to a chilly, cloudless night, he had hardly realized how smoothly the minutes had passed. He had only had to pinch himself a few times to confirm that he was having one of the best nights of his entire life, but even that surprise and wonder was diminishing, instead being replaced by a gentle confidence that his life was going in the right direction. That God had him in His hand.

Zipping up his jacket against an evening chill, he took a deep breath as they emerged onto the sidewalk and began their leisurely stroll back to her apartment.

She talked and he listened. He fed her question after question about her life, her hometown, her little brother, anything that would get those beautiful lips to keep moving so he could follow the melody of her voice, the harmony of her wonderful self.

Christine was laughing at the story she had just told about Darren, her brother. Andy laughed with her, his arm around her as they walked. Looking down at her laughing face he found himself drawn to her and before he knew it he had leaned in and was kissing her. She kissed back, and it surprised Andy that he wasn't more surprised. He hadn't intended to kiss her, it had just happened, as naturally as everything else that had transpired between them that night.

She pulled back from him and with a smile said, "That's a first from you!"

Arms wrapped around each other, he looked down and wondered if what she said was true. Had he really not kissed her yet? And it was true, he hadn't. He had instead let her lead. Partly out of respect for her, and partly out of fear. But here he was, leaning in for more kisses.

"It is a first, and hopefully not the last!" He brought his lips down to hers and they met gently, then urgently. He found her kissing him back hungrily and the realization that she seemed to really want to kiss him, that she was swept away in the kiss stirred a passion in him. It was a passion that he knew lay beneath his interest in Christine but one he had not really connected with yet, not as insistently as he now felt it.

It was powerful, it was wonderful, and it seemed the perfect cap to an amazing night and week.

Finally, their lips broke and Christine caught her breath.

"Mister Harding, I like that you know what you want!" she said, still catching her breath.

He looked at her with more confidence than ever before. "I do know what I want. I want to be with you."

"Me, too," she said, as simple as that. She hugged him, resting her head against his chest. "Me, too."

It was perfect.

Chapter 12

Day six, Way Six. Those were the first thoughts in Andy's head as he woke up. Though it had been hard to fall asleep with thoughts of Christine – and that kiss! – floating through his head, once he was out, he slept soundly. The sleep of angels.

The sunny mood inside him contrasted with the blustery cool of this particular Saturday morning. No joggers out in this weather, he noted. It also meant the little bakery in Kenmore Square would have shorter lines. He headed a few blocks down and over to the little spot fronting what was normally a busy intersection. It seemed Boston had deserted him, yet nothing about this cloudy, abandoned morning could put a dent in his feelings: He was in love and he knew that God was calling him. Two wonderful, powerful, almost mystical things. Perhaps the two most important things that Andy could have hoped for in his time at college. And both were happening at the same time. Yes, sir, no grey skies could dampen his spirits.

He crossed Commonwealth Ave and popped into the little bakery. A kind of faux-European joint, the aroma of deep, rich coffee and fresh-baked pastries was a bit above his normal fare. True to his expectations, the line was short, the few patrons were bundled in jackets and reading newspapers, keeping mostly to themselves. He ordered a hot chocolate and a chocolate croissant – that was way above his normal fare, but it was a special day and he wanted even his breakfast to know it. Soon enough he was out the door, juggling his still-warm croissant and his styrofoam cup of hot chocolate.

Along the few-block walk back up Commonwealth, the clouds made good on their promise of rain, if just slightly at first. This encouraged Andy to finish his pastry before it got soggified by rain.

Now free to use two hands, he clutched his cup of hot chocolate to keep his fingers warm.

Andy had no sooner opened the door to Gordon's building when the clouds unleashed actual rain, pushed at him by the insistent wind. Andy blessed his luck that he made it to the building just in time. He was so happy about this coincidence that he annoyed even himself with how happy he felt.

Taped to Gordon's door was the envelope the professor had promised. Andy pulled down the envelope and was surprised to find it felt rather light in his hands. He had intended to take it away to the library before opening it, where he could make notes as he reviewed it. But his curiosity got the best of him and he slid his finger under the flap and tore it open.

Inside was a single piece of paper. Not even a piece of paper, but a piece of memo paper, like a three-by-five notecard. He lifted it from the envelope and saw just one sentence.

Welcome to Way Six: Find the truth.

Hesitant, Andy looked at the envelope again to make sure he hadn't missed anything. He found nothing. He quickly glanced at the ground in case something had fallen out without him noticing. Nothing again. He turned the memo paper over in his hand and found nothing on the other side. Puzzled, he looked again. Then, numbly, he turned and walked out.

~

He sat in the library reading room overlooking the water of the Charles River. He was still wet from the walk from Gordon's office. The buoyant, rain-avoiding Andy had become a soaked dog while running the few blocks to the library. Now he sat, delaying pulling his things out in hopes that he might dry off a bit before getting his notebooks wet. Looking out the window, sensing the intermittent press of the wind against the large plate glass, Andy could at least take shelter from the elements up here. Outside, he was astonished to see actual whitecaps on the water as a northeastern wind pushed against the flow of the water toward the harbor. The choppy blue of the water rose and fell in quick pulses, the whitecaps disappearing and reappearing in an endless, random cycle.

Finally, Andy could retrieve his notebook and write the words that had puzzled him while making the frantic trip to the library.

Welcome to Way Six: Find the truth.

Isn't that what he had been doing all week? How did trying to do it again constitute a new Way? Flipping back through the pages in his notebook, Andy reviewed the first five Ways:

Way One: Humility.

Way Two: Believe.

Way Three: Create.

Way Four: Follow.

Way Five: Seek.

That's when he saw it. Seek, and ye shall find. He turned back to his newest note, then added below it the more succinct version suggested by the five ways that preceded it.

Way Six: Find.

That was elegant, for sure, but what did it mean? Hadn't Andy already done the finding he needed to do in Way Five? That was the purpose of seeking, after all. And Andy had found some amazing things when he completed Way Five. He found himself in the scriptures, in the form of the Ninevites, which led him to find himself needing the same message they needed. Just rethinking the lesson from the prior day was enough to remind him of the tremendous feelings of hope and faith that had passed through him.

What else was there to find?

He looked back at the piece of paper and his notes. *Find the truth.*

He flipped back through his notes. Truth was the whole point of this exercise. And as he had told Gordon when pressed, Andy wanted *the* truth, not just *a* truth. Yet, by his own notes and his own reflection, he had amassed many truths, all of which were now a vital part of his faith.

Was that what Gordon meant? Add it all up and it will become a single truth? He jotted some notes to think this through.

Humility was necessary to remove any incorrect notions – untruths – from my mind, to prepare me for the truth. I had to forsake my assumptions and be willing to be led to new, better truth.

Believing required me to accept the truth offered at its barest, most basic level. If God said it, I had to be willing to accept it as true, even while allowing Him to have truths in store that were not immediately apparent.

Creating gave me freedom to explain how the truth could have happened in whatever way I could imagine. But I couldn't go beyond the truth or transgress it, even as I expanded my ability to let God make true be true in whatever way He deemed fit.

Following taught me to follow the effect that the truth had on the world. This provides a kind of witness that the truth was indeed true, because the consequences of a truth prove the power of the truth.

Seeking taught me to find my own truth – where I fit in the story of Jonah. It made the story truer for me than it was otherwise.

Five Ways, five different facets to the single gemstone of truth. He truly had accumulated some new understanding and it was, added up, "true" to him. But was it *the* truth he had been looking for? Something didn't feel right. The fact is, all of this started thanks to Pastor Tentworthy's claim that Jonah's story had to be true or everything else in the gospel couldn't be true. It was a pivotal claim and it had turned Andy's world completely upside down.

Could he say, now that so much time and effort had passed, that the Jonah story was true?

The fact was, he still didn't have a *true* answer for how long Jonah was underwater, whether it was a fish or other natural marine animal that swallowed him, or even the details of what Jonah taught the Ninevites. But he had some truth. Was that enough? He flipped back through his notes to Way One, where Gordon had crafted what he called Tentworthy's dilemma:

The story of Jonah is a test of our faith in God's ability to find us, to hunt us down when we oppose Him. That no matter how much we run from Him, He can find us. For in Him is all power! He controls the waves and the winds, He controls even the fishes of the sea. Did

Moses part the Red Sea? Could Jesus rise again after the grave? If we disbelieve Jonah, do we not disbelieve the very Son of God himself?

Gordon had copied down what Andy had told him, modifying it only a little bit, and then telling him that this statement was true. That had felt like a punch in the gut at the time. To which Gordon went on to say that it was true in ways that Andy couldn't see at that point.

The whole exercise of the week, all of the Ways thus far had been designed to help him find the truth. This truth. This statement. If he understood Gordon right, it wasn't the story of Jonah that had to be found true or false, but this statement. Andy thought he was on to something with that train of thought, though he wasn't sure what. The whole week he had spent reading Jonah to find many truths in it, about it, and about himself.

But Way Six seemed to be about finding the truth of this statement. His only impulse was to rewrite the statement, the dilemma, as Gordon had called it, as a series of statements that needed to be tested. He scribbled out the first sentence and looked at it.

The story of Jonah is a test of our faith in God's ability to find us, to hunt us down when we oppose Him.

It had felt like such a dark and condemning pronouncement. At least all through Sunday evening and throughout the sleepless night that led to Monday's bleak sunrise. Andy had felt the heat of God's search for him, a possible faithless unbeliever, someone whose faith might not measure up. He could recall the urge to look over his shoulder, nervous that an angry God was stirring in His heavens, ready to hunt down a weak and trembling Andy.

Across the river the winds had not ceased, rain continued to pelt the window and Andy imagined a chill in the air to match the ferocity of the tempest outside. Or was it the tempest inside? Andy shook that memory off and looked at the sentence again.

Humility, he thought. *What do I think I know about this statement that might not be true?*

First, he knew that God hadn't sought him out vengefully all week. Instead of being thrown to the waves, he had been lifted up, by

Gordon, by scripture, by prayer, by God – and yes, by the joy of Christine in his life. He looked again at the condemning sentence.

The story of Jonah is a test of our faith in God's ability to find us, to hunt us down when we oppose Him.

And there he saw it. *God's ability to find us.* This whole time he had imagined that this referred to Jonah's attempt to flee his call to Nineveh by jumping on the nearest ship going in the opposite direction. God had hunted him down with a storm and a wind and even the casting of the lots by the sailors. That God wanted to punish Jonah for his failings.

But what if – and it took humility to see this and another measure of humility to believe it – what if God was hunting Jonah, not to punish him, but to bring him back.

That no matter how much we run from Him, He can find us.

With his entire world turned upside down, Andy could see it, he could finally see it. The truth! The truth in the story of Jonah was not that God punished Jonah for his doubts. But that God left no stone, no storm, no fish unturned in his effort to find, reach, and ultimately deliver him!

For in Him is all power!

Even as the storm beat upon the windows outside the library, casting a curtain of darkness across Cambridge to the north, Andy's mind couldn't have been clearer, his heart couldn't have been more softened. Enveloped in this warmth of spiritual knowledge, he read on.

He controls the waves and the winds, He controls even the fishes of the sea. Did Moses part the Red Sea? Could Jesus rise again after the grave? If we disbelieve Jonah, do we not disbelieve the very Son of God himself?

That was when Andy began to weep.

He unleashed a torrent, punctuated by thunderous sobs. How had he not seen this before? All this time, had it been his whole life that he had misunderstood this key point? The storm was not a storm of vengeance, it was a storm of grace and love! A storm of longing and seeking, a storm of redemption! There, next to his study table, he collapsed to his knees and let rage the beauty of the storm within.

He did not want this feeling to end even as it ebbed. This truth, it fed his soul like nothing else in this powerful week had. He offered a prayer of thanks from his overflowing heart as the wind inside him slowly, gently subsided. Then he lifted himself back to his seat, took his pencil and wrote:

This is the truth that sets me free.

Free at last, his soul seemed to say. Not just free from sin. Not just free from sorrowful death. The twin corruptions that haunt all of us and which Jesus frees us from. But free from the fear that God longs to punish him for our weaknesses, our doubt, our failings. The awesome power of God is not something to fear and hide from. It is a power to run toward!

It is the power that called Jonah back to the truth that he knew: God is watching you – not as an administrator of punishments but as a loving Father. It is the power that Jonah drew on when he called all of Nineveh to return to God. To be reconciled to His grace and His love, not to be punished.

Even when the love feels harsh!

This is where Andy's mind really connected the dots: God's love, like the embracing hold of the fish around Jonah, may sometimes be hard to endure, it may seem like a kind of death that we have to pass through; there will be moments of darkness and despair, moments when we will need to utterly trust in Him and follow Him.

That is why the story of Jonah is indeed the litmus test of our faith and trust in Jesus Christ. Not because our doubts about Jonah make us unworthy to have faith in Christ as Tentworthy's words seemed to imply. But because our faith in Jonah's tale opens up for us the ultimate truth of the infinite mercy of Jesus Christ.

Andy scribbled furiously as idea after idea lined up neatly in his mind.

Jonah is Jesus in that he was called to save a wicked people in a wicked world that was destined to kill him.

Jonah is Jesus in that he spent three days swallowed in the darkness of death before his mission could be completed.

Jonah is Jesus in that he was "baptized" by water.

Jonah is Jesus in that his message can turn around even the most "evil" of people — his power cannot be stopped. In the words of Tentworthy, "For in Him is all power!"

I am Jonah because I run from the good I have been called to do.

I am Jonah because my own actions cause me to suffer consequences that God allows (or even causes) to befall me.

I am Jonah because I will suffer spiritual death due to my actions and only by calling upon the grace of God in the name of Jesus Christ can I be delivered from the depths of that death.

I am Jonah because I will surely suffer physical death but will be resurrected to face the love of God to the degree that I have prepared myself to accept it.

I am Nineveh because, as Isaiah prophesied, though my sins be as scarlet, they shall be as white as snow!

The entire story of Jonah, a mere four chapters in length, tucked neatly in the Old Testament, summarized in just a few sentences. All of them true.

This story is true! Andy wrote, and underlined it twice with such force that his pencil lead snapped.

Andy's mind and body seemed enveloped in the single, glorious light that filled him. The sun had indeed risen. The storm of love had given way to illumination. Where once there had only been faith, clouded by doubt, there was now truth.

He looked out through the window, across the tempest-tossed waves, and was half surprised that the storm outside had not ceased.

~

The knock at the door was curiously insistent though hard to hear over the gusts and the rain outside.

"Hang on!" Christine called from down the hall. She pushed her sleeves up, glancing at the mirror across the room to make sure her ratty, old sweatshirt didn't hang too open. She hadn't expected anyone.

161

Why would she? It was raining cats and dogs out there, maybe even an elephant or two. Whoever had come over during this storm was certifiably nuts.

The door knocked again and she pushed down a bit of annoyance. She grabbed the handle and turned, half-ready to show her displeasure.

"Yeah—"

There stood Andy, soaking wet and being buffeted by chill winds.

"You! What are you doing out there, get in here!"

She was glad that her initial annoyance converted so quickly into a surprised joy at the sight of him. But then once she got him in the doorway and shut the door behind him, she let him have it.

"Are you nuts?" she started, pounding lightly on his jacket, only to get splashed on in the process. This made her even more annoyed, yet made the whole event seem a bit more playful.

"I'm so sorry!" he began, starting to sweep the excess water from his sleeves and front with his hands.

"Don't do that," she chastised, "here, just take your coat off. Your head! You're going to drip all over the place, wait right there and I'll get you a towel!" She was enjoying the mild disapproval she was showing, hoping that the irrepressible smile on her face would betray her true feelings at having been interrupted in what was otherwise a boring, dreary day.

He dutifully took his coat off by the door, careful not to get water everywhere. She came back from the hall closet with a towel.

"Here, take this," she offered, casting the towel over his head and taking his coat from him gingerly, setting it over the back of a dining room chair she pulled toward the door. It was a value, she figured, of having a small apartment. Everything was within arm's reach.

He finished drying off his head and she reached up to drape the towel over the back of his neck. This gave her an excuse to put her arms on him, which she thoroughly enjoyed. She knew it would unsettle him and she loved making him blush. His pale skin lit up like a sunburned lobster whenever she was forward. She didn't intend to be such a coquette, but such actions just came naturally to her. And around him she was feeling the urge to do them all the time. She had taken some time to analyze this and realized that there was no mystery to it. She liked him. And she liked to fluster him because it made it easy to see that he liked her, too.

She was surprised that it had come so naturally, so quickly. She had dated plenty of fancier boys. And while they were nice – most of them, anyway – none were as unguarded as Andy. None so sincere. Sincerity was in short supply in college, probably in the world. And as Christine had told herself many times, she was a girl who knew what she wanted. She wanted sincerity. In Andy she had found that. And so much more.

As predicted, he flushed a bit with her arms up around his neck. He reached up to enclasp her hands with his, but rather than pull her hands away, he actually tightened his grip, bringing her even closer to him.

He was looking at her intently, eyes not averting, grin not fading. His dripping, drenched self was momentarily unaware of anything but the gentle, generous tension between them.

He really likes me, Christine thought, and it warmed her to know it. *No need to hide anymore. No need to wonder. I have found what I want.*

The thought was fulfilling, encompassing, and it made her happy. She was lost in that thought right up until the moment that he bent down to kiss her.

She kissed back.

His hands let go of hers, running the length of her arms, over her shoulders, down to the small of her waist, and suddenly his long arms engulfed her in the most complete embrace, two arms wrapped around her, two lips pressed against hers – two souls kindling a spark of something wonderful between them.

Their kissing grew intense, then passionate and her happiness grew.

Finally, he pulled away, panting slightly for lack of breath. Her eyes were closed, but she felt the air of his breath on her face as she slowly opened her eyes. The room, though technically deprived of any sunlight from outside, brightened as she looked up at him. Her arms were still wrapped around his neck, and as she withdrew them, she caressed his neck, then rested her palm against his chest. His heart was beating a hundred miles a minute and this thought made her happy.

He spoke, breaking the loving silence between them. "I'm having a wonderful day," he said, elation in his voice.

"You mean even before that kiss?" she grinned up at him wickedly, pushing against his chest as if to say, *get the answer right!*

"That was the icing on an already wonderful cake."

She slid her hand down to his, pulling it away from her waist, though he seemed reluctant to relax his grasp of her. Turning, she led him over to the couch.

"Then you'll have to tell me all about it."

~

Andy looked at his watch. Twenty minutes of sitting on the sofa with Christine, trying to share a week's worth of spiritual growth and it couldn't have gone worse if Andy had deliberately tried to sabotage the conversation.

They had started snuggled together against one arm of the sofa, with her nestled against him, holding one of his hands across her lap, with his other arm around her. Now twenty minutes later, he was still where he started, but she was a few feet away from him. Their hands were no longer touching, his arm was no longer around her.

"Andy, look, don't you see? The things you're talking about, these are all the mistakes that Christians have made for centuries! This certainty you say you have found, it's exactly the root of every moment of Christian hubris, from the crusades to the inquisition to the persecution of the Quakers by the Pilgrims." She was speaking eloquently, passionately, and with strong reasoning. "In every case, the Christians refused to let doubt dissuade them, they insisted on certainty and that certainty led them to persecute and ultimately hunt other people who didn't live up to their certainty!"

A piece of him wanted to admire her – did admire her, actually – for her adept navigation of history, her sincerity. But how could she be so wrong about God while being so good and right in every other way?

He fretted over his words, over his awkwardness there on the couch. Had he really ruined this day's events so quickly? "Christine, I, er, I don't know, maybe I'm not saying it right." Part of him wanted to say, *It's not like I proposed going out to hunt campus agnostics!* But he knew that throwing an emotional argument at her wasn't going to help. He resorted to the only thing he knew.

"All I know is that I feel like God has been trying to tell me something. Something about myself. Maybe something about Himself as well. And I can't well reject something if God wants to tell it to me–"

"I know you don't want to hear this, Andy, but maybe you should." She leaned in, patiently, and free of the exasperation he imagined she felt at this point in the argument. "Well-meaning Christians have believed that God is trying to speak to them for centuries. At worst it leads them to witch hunting, but at best it leads them to embarrassment. How many times did the Seventh-Day Adventists reschedule the second-coming of Christ?"

"That's different," he started.

"Is it?" she shot back. "Isn't this how it starts? First you believe God is trying to speak to you, then you think He has told you something that nobody else knows, then you think that your special knowledge and special relationship with God frees you of the constraints that bind everybody else. That's why there must be doubt because certainty is a road that only leads one way, straight off a cliff."

He was puzzled. Hadn't she said she was a believer? Hadn't she encouraged his studies all this week? He paused, sighed once, then tried to start again.

"But doesn't God want us to know Him?" He wasn't looking at her as he asked his. He was asking the floor, or maybe the air. Based on where he was looking, he was asking his hands, tightly wound together in his lap. *Doesn't He?* Andy asked himself wordlessly.

Christine became more confident even as Andy shrank in doubt. "He wants us to seek Him. He wants us to keep trying to get closer to Him, but because He's a mystery, He keeps moving one step beyond our understanding. We can't ever be certain about Him, but we can keep trying."

It was actually a very beautiful theology, articulated in such a clear manner from a smart woman he respected – and probably loved – and it would have been so easy to just compromise. But he had so recently been driven like a spike into the ground of doubt, despairing hammer blow after despairing hammer blow. Gordon had helped him recover from doubt by promising clarity. Certainty. And what's more, he had found it. The truth. Six different ways, all leading to the same powerful truth. Jesus Christ is the literal savior of the world. He sought me, He redeemed me, *for in Him is all power!*

If you can't be certain of Jesus Christ, of what can you be certain? Tentworthy's dilemma came back to him. And instead of feeling frustrated at the man's implied challenge, Andy now knew that whether the preacher was aware of it or not, he had spoken powerful words that had pointed the way to a certainty Andy could not now walk away from.

"But I don't want that," Andy finally muttered. The words solidified the silence that was forming between them. And for a moment he imagined that he hadn't even said it out loud. He looked up at her. She sat, poised, confident. Loving, even. She wanted him to see the light. She wanted him to come back to her from his flight of fancy, to see the reason and intellect that motivated her.

But he could not. "What if I don't want that?" he asked, this time with increasing volume. "What if I don't want to seek Him forever, never to find anything more than questions that lead to more questions, doubt upon doubt until there's nothing left to believe in?"

"That's what faith is!" Christine responded quickly, emphatically. "That's the whole point of faith and that's why it's hard to keep the faith. But that's also how we are protected from the excesses of supposed certainty and truth."

"But it's the truth that sets us free," Andy began, quietly at first, gradually building steam. "And I want to be free." *Like I am now*, he felt inside.

He regarded her in that moment and saw the beauty and confidence that attracted him to her. Fear came to him, but did not overcome him. This most beautiful week in which he went from imagining he could never approach such a lovely woman to being able to wrap his arms around her – and those kisses! His lips practically puckered at the thought of those delicious kisses. Was he a fool to upset the woman who could bestow such gifts?

Or was he a fool to turn his back on the God who had sought him out through this week of ways?

Christine scooted closer to him, perhaps sensing the resolve building in him. Her very willingness to approach him despite the obvious disappointment she felt meant she felt something for him, didn't it?

"Andy," she began, placing her hand on his for the first time since their disagreement started. He looked at it, while she looked at him. "You faced a difficult trial. A trial of faith and you passed. That's good. It's what makes you a good man – you want to do good things in the world and you want to please God. But look around you, you'll see that there are many ways to please God and all of them require that you decide for yourself what God wants and go make it happen. You want the world to be a better place? Run for mayor of your town, become a banker and donate money to charity, adopt some kids from a war-torn region of the world. All of those things are good – and I," at the word *I* Christine suddenly become more intense, "I want to do those things, too. I want to do them with somebody else who wants to do them, somebody good, somebody like you, Andy."

Now she was genuinely pleading with him. "But you can only get there if you're willing to leave a few question marks in the heavens, question marks that you never get to answer, question marks that you live with knowing that if you tried to answer them, you would answer them wrong and ultimately hurt the people around you."

Her hand was warm on his hand, and it suddenly grew more tender.

"I can't be one of those people," she said, then slowly withdrew her hand. "I told you that I know what I want. But I also know what I don't want."

Andy's heart was breaking. Just an hour before he had stood on top of the world despite the storm surging around him. Now he was lying on the shore, waves pulling at his feet, rain and thunder pummeling him from above.

And these words came to him, in a whisper so potent that it invigorated what had felt like a tired, broken body.

Arise, and go hence.

Driven by a pre-conscious urge, Andy slowly stood, carefully removed the towel from around his neck, folded it and laid it on the arm of the sofa. He walked to the door in measured steps. He withdrew his jacket from the back of the chair and slowly slid into its wet arms. He was aware that she was watching him, but he dared not meet her gaze.

He placed his hand on the door handle, pausing for an instant. Did he hope she would call him back to her?

She didn't.

He turned the doorknob. "Thank you," he said, facing the door. Opening the door, he slipped out into the tempest.

Chapter 13 - Interlude

The man, beaten and bedraggled, lifted himself from the sand. Casting a glance up to a tormented sky, he could only see a raging, potent heaven. Clouds appeared to combine against him, in billowing, pulsing fury. Instead of merely falling, the rain came with force, flung from above, in tiny scourges that bit his flesh as if to draw blood.

Squinting roughly to keep the driving rain from his eyes, the man directed his gaze to the horizon. His goal lay beyond that horizon, in a direction he did not want to go. Beyond that mark on the edge of his vision lay a future that to his thinking just minutes ago was only dismal. No good could be found there.

Or could it? What was the definition of good but to do as God commanded?

Looking down at his hands, unconsciously formed into fists of resilience, the man opened his right palm. There he saw the grit of the sand that clung, wet, to his fingers. Rubbing that grit between his thumb and his fingers, he saw himself for a moment as the storm-driven sand. Like sand, he was unable to move himself, carried instead by the hand of someone larger than he, with greater purpose.

Did he believe in the greater purpose? Looking back up to the horizon, calculating the long march he had ahead of him, he tightened his hand back into a fist.

No, that was wrong. He was not the sand, not at all. He was free to act. The truth had made him free. The truth that God is greater than he, yet God would condescend to invite the man to participate in divine plans. The truth that he was free to accept this grace or reject it. But that God would do everything possible to keep the invitation open as long as necessary.

The man stepped forward, taking the first of many steps toward the unknown horizon and beyond.

"I will accept thy plan and make it my own," he muttered resolutely. "Let us go hence. Let the world know with whom I stand. Because this is not just about me. It's about as many people as I can possibly bring with me."

Only then did the man notice that the wind and rain were moving in the direction he now walked.

Chapter 14

Andy walked with measured steps. The walk from Christine's apartment was perilous in every possible sense. Unexpectedly sharp gusts of wind threatened to pull him off course, driving rain impaired his vision. Had he been tempted to walk his feelings off, he couldn't have done so, not without enduring significant pain.

Part of him wanted to suffer that pain.

What had he done? He had walked away from the only real girlfriend of his entire life. And why? Because she categorically refused to accept his spiritual certainty. It seemed the flimsiest of reasons to end an otherwise ideal relationship. And she had argued with such persuasive power. After all, she wasn't arguing that he should abandon God, merely treat him as unknowable. You could, she insisted, do good things in the world and trust that God would receive you in the end.

He sincerely hoped that she would do all of those things as planned and that God would receive her in the end.

But Andy had a different feeling about what the future would bring. Something told him that his weeklong wrestle with faith in this otherwise unremarkable year of 1987 was just a premonition of a wave of doubt that he and many others would have to fight off some day. The changes he had experienced in his short life – the removal of prayer from school, the arrival of no-fault divorce, the legalization of abortion. He wasn't particularly troubled about these things, or hadn't been. Each one, on its own, he could manage by living a good life and either compensating for or avoiding those things in his own life. Exactly what Christine's religious philosophy would approve of, Andy knew. But he also knew, with a certainty he could not explain, that these social changes weren't the end points in a now-concluded argument. Instead, these were the opening salvos in a protracted cultural battle that Andy perceived this country was committed to waging.

Did he have any reason to expect that the challenges to faith would someday decrease? Not a chance. And when he had finally returned to his dorm room and had been able to close the door to the buffeting winds, he saw Nineveh ahead of him. The Nineveh he realized that was growing all around him was a world devoid of faith where not only would many lose their faith, but those that kept it would struggle to defend themselves against angry, tempestuous voices that would persecute them. And he was already safely swallowed up in its belly.

Andy peeled his wet clothes off and towel dried his hair, pondering this imminent future. He was not an end-is-near kind of Christian. Even growing up under the threat of thermonuclear war Andy had never given into the vague feeling that the world was coming to an end. He still resisted that notion now. Instead, however, he was visualizing a different kind of future. Not an end, brought on by fire or ice. But an end of faith, replaced by a world where television shows would remove faith completely or only include it as a point of mockery. A world where religious people would be shamed for believing in something so "nonscientific" as God. A world where intellectual and political elites would rally together to push the idea of God out of public discourse. These ideas rushed into Andy's mind and he sat down on the edge of his bed struck with how easily this could happen and how certainly it would happen. It was not a question of if, but when. And who. Who would survive this onslaught of pressure, shame, and officially sanctioned persecution.

Andy's mind entered a kind of meditative state where, for the briefest of moments, he even imagined he could see a world where the president of the United States would instruct federal prosecutors to sue churches, convents, and religious schools for failure to support these elites' social goals and methods. And the nation of Nineveh would applaud him.

It was an absurd notion, but Andy couldn't shake it. In that world – that Nineveh – believers would have to have certainty or they could not survive. They could not have mere faith; instead they would require truth. The kind of truth that would set them free, free to resolutely follow God, despite the slings and arrows of the coming persecution. Free to overcome even their own doubts and embarrassment as they fell out of public favor. This truth also needed to be shared with the rising generation, a generation which would only ever know a world of self-indulgence, self-righteous atheism, and self-obsession. Who would tell them that faith was more than just a gentle wish for a heaven that offered more questions than answers?

It humbled him to know just how hard a haul he had ahead of him. Here he had just endured a week of emotional and spiritual turmoil, thinking that he would come out of the other side calm and at peace. Yet now he saw that though the storm was over, the real battle lay ahead. Things would get demonstrably worse, impossible to escape, in a very few short years. He was no longer battling for his own faith, he had an obligation to set others free, too.

With the winds still beating on his dorm window, Andy arose from his bed, clenched his fists and set his jaw before saying aloud, "I will stand with God, come what may."

~

Sunday morning came and even as the night passed, so did the storm. Andy had slept contentedly, as if storing up energy for the task ahead.

He arose and prepared for church. The walk to Marsh Chapel was bright and beautiful. Fallen branches and leaf-cluttered gutters gave testimony of the prior day's tempest, but the testimony that remained was that light will emerge, the storm will end, and Sunday will come.

When he arrived, he looked up at the imposing Gothic structure of Marsh Chapel. The deep blue of a summer morning stood behind the entry and its three spires.

Andy was happy. The majestic organ played inside, its music welcoming the light stream of congregants filing in through the entry doors.

Within minutes, Andy would join them, would pray with them. And pray for them. He was not a prophet, but he felt he had been given a moment of prophesy. The vision he had had the night before would surely come to pass and everyone in attendance today, everyone who partook of the emblems of communion, would soon be faced with a choice. He prayed that each would have the faith to let God find them, just as he had let God find him this past week. That everyone would be, just as Jesus had prayed, one, united in this truth: *That the world may believe that Thou hast sent me.*

For this powerful new awareness of his own relationship with God and for what he now understood would be a lifelong effort to heal Nineveh, he had Pastor Tentworthy to thank. The irony made him grin as he confidently stepped forward toward the chapel doors.

~

The brilliant sunlight of morning had persisted throughout the day, giving Andy the welcome opportunity to have the long walk he would have wanted to have yesterday. Instead of this walk being the one that helped him clear his mind after his conversation with Christine, this was the walk where he looked afresh at the world, aware of its predicament as if for the first time. Nineveh. A wonderful, beautiful, but lost place. And likely to become even more lost in the days and years ahead.

Eventually the time came to join Gordon in his office for their afternoon check-in. He had made it through this week of extreme trial. It took him Six Ways to get to this specific Sunday, but all six led to the same truth. And now, possessing it, Andy could barely recall the frightened doubt that had plagued him just a week ago. What's more, he was different in how he interacted with his mentor. Gone were his own self-conscious hesitations, replaced by a resolve that Andy hadn't known he lacked.

He recited all the events that had transpired since they last met. Gordon listened carefully, nodding here, taking notes there. And when Andy finished with the summary of the feelings he had that morning as he prepared to take communion buoyed up by the new truth that sustained him, he was less concerned about what Gordon was thinking, less preoccupied with whether he had impressed the good professor. Instead, he was sharing the light and grace that had come to him with a fellow Christian. One whom Andy respected and hoped to learn from, but a fellow believer nonetheless.

When he had finished, Gordon paused, looking intently, searchingly at Andy. Then, in his insistent, knowing way, the professor leaned forward in his chair. Thus poised to speak, he still held his tongue for a moment. And that's when Andy realized that his beloved professor was struggling to speak through evident emotion.

Finally, with a slight tremor in his voice, Gordon said, "Andy, you finally have it."

More words were not necessary. Though Andy would have struggled to define exactly what Gordon meant, the feeling behind it was one that they shared in that moment. It was a growing sense of spiritual elation mixed with a firm commitment to follow God wherever He would lead.

Andy found himself also trembling with emotion. There was something of eternity in the feeling that passed between them and Andy suddenly understood why Professor Gordon had spent so much time investing in him these past few days. Gordon had obviously learned the lesson of Jonah, of Nineveh, and of God's irrepressible, inescapable love years ago. And he had made a similar promise to himself and to God to share it wherever possible.

So, with tears welling in his eyes, Andy acknowledged the gift and its giver with a shaky voice. "Thank you, professor, for giving it to me."

Epilogue

Now all these years later, Andy leafed through his journal. His entry from that day's conversation with Gordon was brief. And it was followed up by many entries from that summer of work at the man's side. There was, indeed, much wisdom left to be gained from the man, even still today. The last bit of knowledge he recorded on that day, however, had been this simple restatement of Tentworthy's dilemma.

> *The story of Jonah is a test of our faith in God's desire to find us,*
> *to seek us out when we turn away from Him. That no matter how much*
> *we turn from Him, He can and will call for us. For in Him is all power!*

Andy re-read it for the first time in many years. It had once been so crucial to his thinking, to his motivation, that he had memorized it word for word. By now, however, Andy realized some time had elapsed since he considered every word. *For in Him is all power!*

He regretted that elapsed time. A time during which he had neglected the power of the Six Ways that had led him to One Truth. And his more recent neglect of that One Truth had had significant consequences for him. Consequences he now had to repair.

Fortunately for him, God had the power to help him repair what he had done, to redeem him from himself, and set him back on the path to help the people of Nineveh. People whom God would continue to seek out, though by now, Andy had seen nearly an entire generation turn from Him.

He can and will call for us.

Thankfully, thought Andy, and sighed. He closed his journal and placed it back on the shelf. Then he closed his fists, gripping tightly as if to save himself from being dragged under, and resolutely stepped out of his home office to speak with the woman who, second only to Jesus Christ, had been and would be his salvation.